MERRIOL AND THE LORD HYCARBOX

JENNIFER HASHMI

ILLUSTRATIONS BY
FLOYD RYAN YAMYAMIN

AuthorHouse™ UK
1663 Liberty Drive
Bloomington, IN 47403 USA
www.authorhouse.co.uk
Phone: 0800.197.4150

Published by AuthorHouse 09/26/2016

ISBN: 978-1-4918-8992-3 (sc)
ISBN: 978-1-4918-8993-0 (e)

Print information available on the last page.

Any people depicted in stock imagery provided by Thinkstock are models,
and such images are being used for illustrative purposes only.
Certain stock imagery © Thinkstock.

This book is printed on acid-free paper.

authorHOUSE®

FOREWORD

In the title the name of the Lord of the Earth is Hycarbox. The stories are meant to suggest that consciousness is not separate from the universe, and that morality affects the state of the planet.

The stories show every little creature and every little child, (in fact every human being), being known and cared about in some supra-planetary dimension. They also show help being available to every soul, human or animal, in a very intimate and personal way.In the stories the Lord of the Earth has an envoy, Merriol, who travels between himself and the people of the Earth.When there is some matter which needs attention Merriol is sent as an intermediary to attend to it.

MERRIOL AND THE SCHOOL CHILDREN

Earth's sun was sinking in the West. The sky there gleamed like copper, fading towards the East into misty purple. A crescent moon had appeared. Some looked up to partake again of these recurring mysteries. Others went about their business.

Somewhere within these realms where men cannot go by sea or air dwelt Hycarbox, Lord of the Earth. This was he who was hidden in the snowflakes and the fire, in the elephant and the bumble-bee, the mountains and the rivers and sea, and in the bodies of human beings. Some called him Nature. Some called him Environment.

Though we could not see him who lived in Ever Ever Land there were those who could see him face to face. They could see the beauty of his countenance, know the sweetness of his breath, and hear the melody of his voice. Such a one was Merriol, a servant and messenger of the great Lord. This particular evening he returned to the Lord's feet depressed by all he had seen that day.

"O Lord of the Earth," he said, "I am troubled by what I see on Earth. Everywhere men and women take what they can get for themselves at the cost of others. You have shown them how Nature works in a harmonious interaction of all the parts. They do not learn from what they see. They try to grab for themselves and do not remember that they do not have a planet each. They forget that this one planet and all that is on it has to be shared."

The Lord of the Earth sighed deeply.

I too am troubled, but they are children yet. Perhaps they will learn wisdom before it is too late."

"But when Lord? There is so little time left."

"If they are worthy to possess the Earth they will learn in time. If not they will destroy it. Or maybe I will destroy it for them to put them out of their misery, if that becomes necessary."

"Can you not go to warn them?"

"I already warn them in many ways but they don't want to hear."

"The Lord Money dwells in many homes. They know him well."

"Yes. He does indeed have much influence. He grants a lot of power to those who worship him, so he is popular. No-one sees he is just a fraud. He appears in gold and silken raiment and he talks big. They are deceived. He steals from most of the population to win himself the few. Those few wield his power and make him Lord of the Earth, he thinks! But even he has only the resources of the one planet at his disposal to distribute, so his followers end up fighting. He was a liar from the beginning."

"But if you were to strike those who worship him with but a hair of your head they would be destroyed. Who can withstand the power of your lightening?"

"True, but men and women are not my puppets. They have to choose for themselves. My gifts are free. They do not have to worship me for the sun to rise or the rain to fall, and the fruits of the Earth are abundant if no-one is greedy. A mature man or woman does not grab. Shall I strike many because some are greedy?"

"But Lord, to learn to share they have to learn to love!"

"Yes. And love multiplies itself as money never can. Love is the harmonious inter-action of human hearts. It is the true wealth which can supply all their needs, but it cannot fill hearts that are closed. and they are afraid to open their hearts. They are children................ And gold glitters you see."

"So they prefer the Lord Money."

"Yes. They do. But there are a few hearts which are mine. Earth is not lost yet!"

"Lord I will show you a problem I discovered today."

"By all means show me."

Merriol opened his tunic to display his chest. The events of the day recorded in his heart were there visible to the Lord. The Lord watched the sequence of events, as Merriol thought them over, displayed in his chest like a T.V. screen.

Three young boys aged about eight were huddled together in a corner of the playground of their school. They were taking money from their pockets and discussing it. One boy, Manoj, was saying.

"I had to search in my Mother's kitchen drawer where she keeps the milk money. I asked her for ten rupees to bring to school but she wouldn't give me any more. She gave me ten yesterday."

"I got mine from my Dadi-ji today," said his friend Sumit. "But I don't know what I'll do tomorrow because Mummy and Papa won't give me any more." He showed the others the five-rupee note.

"Ravi said I was to be sure to bring the full twenty today because I couldn't manage any yesterday," said Madan. "I had to take it from Papa's pocket. I don't know what he'll say when he finds twenty gone."

At that moment a much bigger boy aged about fourteen approached them. It was Ravi.

"Where's my money?" he demanded. The younger boys held out the notes.

"Only thirty-five!" exclaimed Ravi. "I need at least fifty. Five isn't enough," he told Sumit. Sumit began to cry. Ravi grabbed his hair till Sumit was screaming. No adult was in sight, and none of the other children felt like interfering, it seemed.

"Right Sumit," said Ravi, letting go. "I want twenty from you tomorrow or you know what will happen!"

"No! No Ravi……. Please……… where can I get all that money?"

"That's your problem." And Ravi walked off.

The Lord of the Universe then saw what the boys could not see. Merriol was there, a fourth in the group, telling the boys to report Ravi to the school principal.

"I wish we could tell the principal," said Manoj.

"That's what I was thinking," said Madan.

"Ravi's father has a very bad temper," said Sumit. "Do you remember how he came shouting at Vinod Choudhary when he beat up Ravi?"

"Pooh. Principal Sir won't be afraid of Ravi's father," said Manoj.

"Maybe not but I am, "said Sumit. "Suppose Ravi's father found out who had reported Ravi to the principal."

"Yes," said Madan. "And Ravi's father is very rich."

The bell rang for the end of recess so the boys returned to their class without having come to a decision."

"You see?" said Merriol to the Lord of the Universe. "What can we do to save these boys? It's true that Ravi's father can cause trouble for people if he wants. Even to the school. It makes Ravi himself feel powerful."

The Lord of the Universe pondered within himself for a moment.

"Merriol," he said. "Go tonight to Ravi's bedroom and report back to me what he is thinking."

"Yes Lord."

In a moment Merriol was winging away through the night. Ravi lived in a first-floor flat in a superior residential area. Merriol found Ravi by himself sitting on his bed looking disconsolate. He was thinking about three of his class-mates. They had suggested bunking school next day because there was a good film on at a cinema in the town. These boys were the sons of factory owners and always had a lot of cash in their pockets, more in fact than had the factory workers themselves. These boys had said they should go to a posh restaurant first where they sold pizzas and hot chocolate fudge. They would have lunch there and then go to the cinema. Then afterwards they could have an ice-cream treat, Ravi knew that all this could not cost less than a hundred rupees, and he had in his pocket only what Sumit, Manoj, and Madan had given him, much less than what he needed. His father gave him Rs. 500 a month but he spent much more than that. How could he admit to his friends that he did not have enough money!

They despised boys without money and ignored them. Money was necessary to have friends, at least friends one respected. He didn't want poor boys for friends. What was he to do? His father kept a lot of money in a secret compartment under the floor of his wardrobe in his bedroom. How about getting some of that? In the normal way it was quite easy to open, if the wardrobe itself was not locked. The servants did not know about it, but he had once seen it by chance when his father was putting notes into it. He did not know Ravi had seen. No-one knew he knew about it. Supposing he went along to his parents' bedroom just now? If they saw his he could think of an excuse, but they were watching a serial on T.V. in the sitting room. He decided to try. He put on his dressing-gown with the deep pockets and went into the room next door where his parents slept. Good! The cupboard was unlocked. With pounding heart he quietly opened the door and rootled among the shoes in the bottom of the cupboard for the wooden panel which lifted out. It was designed to look like the rest of the flooring of the cupboard. He found the tiny crack which enabled one to lever up the panel, and in a moment the compartment was open! Inside was a metal box and when he opened it he found bundles of hundred rupee notes. He hadn't time to start counting out notes, so he took a whole bundle, slipped it into his dressing-gown pocket, replaced the panel and the shoes, closed the wardrobe and fled back to his bed. He'ld done it! Hurray! He must have supplied himself for weeks!

Merriol flew with saddened heart back to Ever-Ever Land. The Lord of the Universe was waiting for him.

"Well? And what did you see?" he asked. Merriol opened his tunic to display for the Lord the events he had witnesses in Ravi's house.

"Does this at least mean he won't harass Sumit, Manoj, and Madan?" he asked.

"We shall see," said the Lord. "Maybe there will be some relaxation for a while but it won't take him long to use up that bundle. His father will be very angry when he discovers money is missing."

Merriol was responsible for overseeing the whole world but he gave special attention to these four boys for the next few days. Poor Sumit produced twenty rupees the following day, having told his mother he needed it for a free for a day trip from school. He hated lying to his mother but if he told her the truth she wouldn't give him the money and she couldn't protect him from the punishment Ravi meted out to those who didn't pay up, which was to steal a copy full of class notes or homework from one's school bag and destroy it. A second failure meant two copies and so on. Sometimes he kept the copy till you gave him the money. You got into trouble from the teacher and at home, and had all the notes to copy out again. Once Madan had told the teacher that Ravi had stolen it. The teacher had called Ravi and he had looked amazed. Since it was impossible to prove Ravi had taken the copy Madan had been punished. The teacher had told him not to tell foolish lies, and in any case if he looked after his school-bag properly other people wouldn't be able to steal from it. Afterwards Madan had been beaten up by Ravi.

So that day Madan, Manoj, and Sumit all had their twenty rupees. Ravi felt the extortion should continue in order to build up supplies for the future. Meanwhile his father had seen that a wad of notes was missing. Ravi had listened that morning from his own bedroom, fearful what would happen. He had hidden his notes in the bed box in his room. Ravi's father in a rage had called out to his mother.

"Madhu! Come here!"Madhu had hurried through from the kitchen, wiping her hands on a small towel.

"Madhu what do you mean by helping yourself to my money!" thundered Ravi's father. His mother had burst into tears though she knew nothing about the money. She was always in trouble for something, but not usually anything so serious. Usually it was because Ravi's father did not like the dinner, or his shirt wasn't well-pressed, or some misdemeaner of that sort. Angry words were nothing new in their home. Ravi's father assumed she had taken the money because she was the only person who was supposed to know about it. A big row had followed. His mother said this was the last straw, and she couldn't put up with any more of his tyranny. She had started to pack her bag. Ravi appeared at the door of their bedroom horrified. What would he do if his mother left them? The thought of telling his father he had taken the money passed through his mind but he dismissed it. He was good at handing out punishment to those weaker than himself, but he was a coward when it came to facing punishment himself. Madhu saw her son watching her, his mouth open in dismay, and thought briefly of taking him with her. Then she thought better of it. How would she be able to support Ravi? She would be a woman in disgrace and without funds. Until she could get a job she would have to depend on her parents. Ravi's fees alone were a big expense. She closed her suitcase and kissed the boy as she passed, tears in her eyes, telling him to be a good boy, and in a minute she was gone.

"And good riddance!" said Ravi's father to cover up his own dismay. He spoke more roughly than he knew, and hardly realized how he terrified his family. He sat on his bed and surveyed Ravi.

"She'll come back," he said in a softer tone. "She's just angry, that's all. She'll come back, you'll see."

"Did she really take the money Papa?" asked Ravi.

"Well I don't know. Perhaps she didn't. Maybe I was too hasty. I am sometimes. No-one else knew about it as far as I know though."

"But why would she take it? You give her money."

"Well I just thought she might have seen some expensive sari she liked - something like that. But maybe she didn't."

"Should we go and say you're sorry?" suggested Ravi.

"Certainly not! I'd lose all respect. She'll come and say she's sorry herself in a little while, you'll see. Then I'll give her money for a sari and that will make her happy. Now run along. It's nearly time for your bus."

"But I haven't got my lunch."

"Well neither have I. We'll have to manage without today."

That morning in the Super Bazar Sumit's mother met Manoj's mother and they stopped to talk about their sons' progress.

"But Sumit can be so careless," complained Mrs. Malik. "He lost his Hindi exercise books not long ago and had to copy out all the work again. With that on top of his homework he was up till two in the morning."

"Manoj is just the same," said Mrs. Puri. "He lost his Social Studies exercise books. It was just before exams too. He didn't have the notes he needed and had to waste study time copying out the notes and then failed his maths as a result. His father was very angry."

"Where's this trip to?" asked Mrs. Malik. "When they're organizing class outings they should send round proper information instead of just sending a verbal message asking for twenty rupees. When I asked Sumit where they were going he didn't even know."

"Class outing?" asked Mrs. Puri. "I haven't heard about that, Manoj never asked for twenty rupees. I suppose he forgot."

"Well Sumit doesn't even know what day it will be!"

"I'll ask Manoj this afternoon."

That afternoon Manoj faced the question of the class outing. He knew what his mother was talking about because Sumit had told Madan and himself about the lie he had had to tell at home. They'ld all had to tell lies because of Ravi, and Manoj didn't want to let Sumit down. At least they had the comfort of suffering shared. It was painful to have to share another lie though. But he couldn't tell the truth. It he did his mother would be on the phone to Sumit's mother in a moment.

"Oh…. er, yes," he said.

"Honestly Manoj, your memory's hopeless! I'll give you the twenty rupees now and you put it safety in your school-bag. Where are you going?"

"Er – we haven't been told yet."

"You mean they've organised this trip which is going to cost twenty rupees, but they don't know where it's to?"

"They haven't told us."

In his home in Shanti Nagar Madan was in deep trouble. He had had to steal another twenty rupees, this time from his mother's purse. His mother had noticed she was twenty rupees down because she kept a careful account. She spoke of it to his father who pricked up his ears, remembering the twenty rupees he had lost. They were not like Ravi's parents. They both worked hard and were honest and self-respecting. They shared the work in the house and they shared their money and spoke courteously to each other. They discussed the lost money with some foreboding. The only solution was that Madan must have taken it. The woman who washed the dishes was never left alone.

Madan, passing by the door of the kitchen, heard their sad discussion. He was filled with shame and self-disgust, and also terror of facing disgrace. Without stopping to think he slipped out through the front door, round the corner of the house, and down the road. He had run away! Anything rather than face the disappointment in his parents' eyes. He kept walking at top speed. Where was he to go? The railway-station! That was where one could pass the day without anyone taking any notice. There were crowds of people coming and going and sleeping in the entance hall. He'd sit there and think what to do.

Merriol hurried back to the Lord of the Universe at lunch time with his tales of woe, his chest so heavy with their burden he felt his heart would break. The Lord saw the events of the morning with deep sorrow.

"And why have they all got themselves into this mess?" he asked Merriol.

"Because of greed?" suggested Merriol.

"Greed yes. And what else?"

"Cowardice," said Merriol.

"Yes Merriol, cowardice. They're all afraid to face the truth. Send my child Minnie to poor Madan squatting by himself in the railway station. She can be naughty but she has the heart of a warrior."

"Yes Lord."

Merriol sped on his lightening wings to the house of Minnie Mehta. Her Cha-cha and Cha-chi were to arrive that day by a lunch time train from Hyderabad. Merriol went along in their car to the station so that he could lead Minnie to Madan. She was a very excited little girl because she loved her father's brother and his wife who were coming to stay with them for a week. All sorts of outings had been planned and it was going to be a very happy time. When they reached the station Mr. Mehta parked the car. They were surrounded by coolies they didn't need as they had only come to meet someone. The three of them hurried in through the station entrance and Mr. Mehta went to get the platform tickets. Mrs. Mehta then caught sight of a neighbour of theirs standing with her suitcase about to go and catch the train which was due to leave. She hurried towards the lady and Merriol caught Minnie's hand and led her away to Madan who was sitting on the ground leaning against a pillar. Merriol blew a mist of forgetfulness into the mind of Mrs. Mehta so that for the moment she would take her attention off Minnie, and he pointed out to Minnie the small boy not much bigger than herself dressed in school-uniform and trying not to cry. Minnie went and squatted down beside him.

"Hello," she said.

"Hello," he answered, and sniffed.

"Can't you find your mummy?" she asked.

"Yes of course I can."

"Well where is she? Why are you sitting here all by yourself?"

"She's not here at the moment but I'm a big boy. I can sit here by myself for while."

"Are you catching a train?"

"I don't know. I might."

"You don't know? How is that?"

"I just came to the station and I was trying to decide what to do next."

"You mean without your parents?"

"Yes. I'm older than you are."

"Not much older. Do your parents know you're here?"

".........No."

"But won't they be very worried wondering where you are?" My parents would be frantic if I just wandered off like that."

"Well you just have wandered off haven't you? Where are your parents?"

"They're here. Daddy's just getting the platform tickets."

"Oh. Well don't tell them about me."

"Have you run away from home?"

"Yes."

"Why?"

"There was some trouble. You do ask a lot of questions."

"I'm interested. You mean you're running away because you're in trouble?"

"........ Yes."

"Well I may be younger than you, but I'm not such a cowardy – custard.

Goodness, I broke our T.V. screen last week."

"What did you do?" breathed Madan, awed at such criminality in such an innocent-looking little girl.

"Well I did cry a bit. I'ld been playing that I was a princess and I climbed on to a chair to address my subjects and the chair wobbled over and crashed into the screen. I fell on the floor."

"Your parents must have been furious. Did you say the servant did it?" Minnie looked shocked.

"We don't have a servant, but if we did how could I be so mean? Mummie was sleeping but I went to tell her quickly to get it over with."

"What did she say?"

"She said I was careless which of course was true."

"What was your punishment? "

"Well there wasn't a special one. We can't watch T.V. for some time. That's the punishment. The repair or buying a new T.V. will be very expensive. So my punishment is feeling bad because Mummie can't see her favourite serials. She said never mind, but I do mind of course. And my cha-cha and cha-chi are just coming and there won't be any T.V. for them either. What have you done wrong? What are you running away for?"

"I stole some money................"

"Oh............. That was very bad."

"Yes I know."

"But if you tell your Mummy and Papa they will forgive you, and you will promise not to do it again. Why run away? Children make mistakes sometimes. Even big people do."

"I know, but they would be so ashamed of me. I don't want to see that."

"Yes but," began Minnie, squatting down besides him near the pillar, "you're only a child. They may want you to be all sorts of good things, but sometimes you're going to be bad things too. Can't you just say you're sorry and promise not to do it again, and don't? Then they'll be proud that you had the courage to speak the truth and to do better."

"It's not as simple as that..................." Slowly Madan explained the saga to Minnie, and the reasons why he had felt forced to do things he was ashamed of. Minnie was very sympathetic. There were bullies in her school too, so she knew the sort of boy Ravi would be. But her reaction was brisk.

"And you daren't tell your parents about Ravi?"

"No."

"That's because you're a cowardy-custard. You can't sit here all night till people ask what you're doing and your parents think you've been kidnapped. Just go home and tell them the whole thing."

"Even about Ravi?"

"Exspecially about Ravi of course. He's got to be stopped hasn't he? You can do that if you can face up to a bit of shame and awkwardness."

"And what about Ravi's father?"

"Would your father be afraid of Ravi's father?"

"Of course not!"

"Well then what are you worried about? Tell your Papa properly what's going on and he'll sort it out. You can't stop Ravi tearing up your exercise books because you aren't big enough. How many exercise books do you intend to copy out again, to have torn again? Anyway, if you're just going to be a cowardy-custard you'll always be in some sort of mess. Oh - Mummie's looking for me. Bye-bye." And she skipped off.

Madan felt braced by this encounter. Just as Ravi had made him feel weak, she had made him feel strong. He thought of her going quickly to tell her mother about the T.V. "to get it over with". Yes, that's what he should do. And going quickly was a good policy. Do what he had to do without pausing to wonder if he dare! So he got up, brushed the dust off his clothes, and headed for home. When he got there his mother was on the phone, but when she saw him she dropped the receiver.

"Oh Madan," she said putting her arms round him, "where've you been! She called out, "Madan's back!" His father came hurrying through from the kitchen.

"Madan!" he cried running towards him.

"Papa I stole that money," said Madan quickley. "I stole twenty rupees from your pocket and twenty rupees from Mummie's purse." And then he cried.

'Madan!" exclaimed his mother pulling him down on to the sofa beside her and holding him. "Poor Madam, what happened darling?" His father came to his other side and held his hand, and between sobs he told them the whole miserable story. When he had finished his mother soothed him and his father dabbed his tears with his hankie.

"Now don't worry about this anymore son," he said. "Sometimes these things happen at school, and in other places too for that matter, but we're proud you could come and tell us all about it. What are we here for if not to help when there's trouble? Don't worry any more about the money. We quite understand. We'll see to this."

That night Madan went to bed a happy boy for the first time for weeks, and vowed to himself that he'ld never be a "cowardy-custard", as the little girl had called him, again.

Merriol, who had remained at Madan's side until he was safely back with his parents, returned to report progress to the Lord of the Universe.

"So the tide has turned," said the Lord Hycarbox. "In the morning go to Sumit's home before he goes to school. Trouble is brewing there."

The next morning Madan asked his parents if he could speak to Sumit and Manoj on the phone himself, so they said he could. Sumit meanwhile was facing the question of the school outing. He had tried to answer his mother's questions without adding more lies to the story, but he was uneasy, and his mother had begun to suspect the truth, Madan's call came when Sumit was trying to think of where the trip could be scheduled for.

"Sumit," said Madan, "I told my parents all about it yesterday. You do the same."

"But……………. But I can't Madan………….. How can I tell them I've told all those lies to……"

"It just needs a tiny bit of courage – you have to do it quickley without stopping to think if you dare," and Madan replaced the receiver the receiver. Sumit started at the phone for a moment. By now Merriol was at his side.

"Go on," urged Merriol," tell them. You admire He-man and Tarzan, and heros like them. Now it's your turn to be a hero. Go quickley." Sumit straightened his back and went through to the kitchen.

"Mummy," he said, "there isn't a school trip. A boy called Ravi makes us give him money every day, so we have to get it somehow. If we don't give him twenty rupees he takes our exercise books and tears them up as punishment, so I had to get the twenty rupees somehow, so I told you there was a school trip but there isn't. And sometimes I've had to tell other lies to get the money." He stood braced for the shock of what his mother would say. She looked at him, stunned for a moment.

"Oh Sumit!" she said after a moment. "How terrible for you! We'll have to report this at school."

"But Mummy, then Ravi will beat us up, or his father will get us into trouble. His father gets very angry."

"Well so do we if someone hurts you! Don't worry Sumit. We'll see to it. Never hide things from us again though, will you dear? It's far too much worry for you."

"No Mummy."

"Stay at home today till we've had time to deal with Ravi. I'll tell your father in a minute."

Merriol knew without having to consult Lord Hycarbox that his place now was with Manoj. Madan had just spoken to him on the phone and he was standing by his phone in a state of indecision. His mother came to tell him to hurry up as it was nearly time to go to school.

"And don't forget to give that twenty rupees to your teacher." she said.

"Tell her," whispered Merriol. Manoj braced himself. He felt he was about to fall off a precipice, but he took the plunge "without thinking" as Madan had advised.

"Mummy there isn't any school trip. Sumit said that because he and Madan and I have to find twenty rupees every day to give to a boy called Ravi. That's why I've had to keep asking for money. And Mummy once I took the milk money from the kitchen drawer. If we don't give Ravi his money he punishes us. He twists our ears or hits us. Sometimes he steals a exercise books and tears it up and we have to get a new one and do the work all over again. You remember I lost my Social Studies exercise books? Well Ravi had taken it because I couldn't give him twenty rupees. We tried telling the teacher once and she called Ravi but he acted so well she didn't believe us and thought it was a lie to get out of trouble." During this recital Manoj's mother stared in amazement.

"But this is terrible!" she exclaimed. "Why didn't you tell me before? And he's taking money like this from Sumit and Madan too?"

"Yes. Madan just rang to say he'ld told his parents so I thought I'ld tell you. We didn't know what to do. If we get Ravi into trouble his father will get us into trouble. After all he will believe Ravi."

"Don't worry about Ravi," said his mother grimly. "I'll just speak to Sumit's mother. Wait here a minute." She had a short conversation with Sumit's mother during which they agreed to meet later in the morning, and they agreed the boys should stay at home that day.

Satisfied with this part of the morning's work Merriol went on to see others in need. That night when he returned to Ever-Ever Land the Lord of the Universe expressed gratification with the progress so far.

"Tomorrow see what Sumit, Madan, and Manoj's parents have done about the situation, and then we will attend to Ravi. Send my son Aman to him. His father is also a child of mine, open to me for the gifts that only I can give. He is now working for the U.N. on problems of world environment and ecology. Currently he is in India. Send his boy Aman to Ravi."

"Yes Lord."

So the next morning Merriol went first to Madan's house. Madan's mother was talking to Madan.

"Last night as you know Manoj's parents and Sumit's parents came here to discuss Ravi. We decided that the three fathers would see Ravi's father today. He will be told that Ravi's harassment must stop, or the three of them will go to the principal of the school. We think that this will be sufficient, but if Ravi gives you any further trouble tell us immediately."

In his house in Modi Nagar Ravi had to face his father's wrath. His father wanted to know where the five hundred rupees he gave him every month went to that he had to beg for sixty rupees each day from other children. What did he do with the sixty rupees a day? Ravi couldn't admit to bunking school. He did say it was necessary to show your friends you were big by treating them in a lavish way and pretending you had more money than they had. Then they respected you. Otherwise he would have only poor children for friends, and he would be reduced to spending his free time playing football or cricket in the park. His father said what was the matter with that? That was how he had spent his own free time when he was a boy, and he had enjoyed every minute of it, and anyway it would help Ravi get off some of his spare fat. It was true that through over-eating and under-exercise Ravi was stout, but Ravi said times had changed and what counted now was money. As Ravi's father also half-believed this theory he had little to say in answer, but he was shocked to see the results of his own philosophy in his son. Ravi must have been listening to him in conversation with other men sometimes. But what Ravi didn't know was that the two men his father counted as his real friends were teachers who could not afford an expensive life-style and were unhappy in posh hotels. Ravi's father enjoyed a cup of tea with them sometimes, and the chance to relax with people for whom he did not have to show off. How could he explain to Ravi that his showing–off was largely acting in order to promote his business? He shook his head. So with a warning to Ravi not to take any more money from other children, and get some exercise, he told him to get ready for school.

However their home without Ravi's mother was not running well and Ravi's uniform was not ready. Exasperated, his father shouted at the servant and told Ravi to stay at home. He had to be off in half an hour.

Later in the morning Ravi wandered disconsolately in the park, and it was here that Merriol brought Aman looking for different types of butterflies. Ravi saw him peering under a bush.

"What are you looking for?" he asked.

"There was a pale blue butterfly with a sort of delicate brown design on it. I was trying to see where it went."

"What for?"

"I like butterflies. I keep a record of each new one I see and draw it. I've got a book on them so I can find it in the book and write the page number by the drawing."

"What for? Is it some sort of competition?"

"Oh no. It's just a hobby."

"You do all that work for nothing?"

"Well it's not really nothing. I like butterflies so I do it for fun. Like some people do bird-watching. I do a bit of that too."

"Why aren't you at school?"

"We had Founders' Day yesterday at school so they gave us a holiday today. Why aren't you at school?"

"My uniform wasn't ready."

"Your uniform wasn't ready? Is your mother sick?"

"No................... she ran away."

"...................... Oh... I'm sorry."

"What's your name?"

"Aman. What's yours?"

"Ravi. What else do you do besides looking for butterflies and birds?"

"Well I'm taking taequondo lessons. There's a group of us. On the evenings when there isn't a taequondo lesson we play football or volley ball in the Sports Complex. Whle I'm in India I'm learning to play the tabala too."

"Don't you always live in India?"

"No. My father travels around. I'm in class nine now though so probably I'll finish my schooling here. What does your father do?"

"He's in business."

"Are you interested in sport?"

"Yes…. But I don't play much."

"There's a lot of homework, but I do some sort of sport every day. Why don't you come and join the Sports' Complex? They're boys like us so you get nice company."

"Well. I might."

"Next holiday my father's taking a party of us to Garhwal. He's working on an aforestation project and they've got a "Plant a Tree" programme.

Government is financing a lot of it but there's a huge area to be planted. Partly as an educational programme they're inviting people to 'plant a tree'. You go and buy a sapling from their nursery and they show you where to plant it. You can put your name on a notice beside it if you want."

"And then it's your tree?"

"Oh no. Human beings have been too greedy, as you will have been reading about at school, so the idea is we give back to Nature a bit of what we have stolen from her. It's a free gift of course, like Nature's gifts are free. So Papa goes quite often. We plant a tree and then we camp for a few days, cooking our own food on a little stove and sleeping out. Papa knows a lot about wild life so we go trecking, and he shows us animals and plants and insects, and we take our lunch in little packs."

Unaccountably Ravi felt close to tears.

"It must be a lot of fun," he said. Aman felt sorry for this lonely boy whose mother had left him.

"You come with us on our next trip," he said impulsively. "Papa will be glad to have you. He loves having new people to show things to, and camping's great. Do you play any instrument? In the evenings we light a fire and play our instruments and sing. Like the cowboys used to."

"No I can't play anything. I'll ask my father if I can have some lessons. Will there be room in your father's car?"

"We go by train and then the local bus and walking. It's more fun that way, and it means more people can join in. What's your address? I'll give you mine and then we can meet again. The best thing will be if you join the Sports Complex and then you'll be in my group."

"I'd like to………….. if my Papa will let me."

"I'll ask my Papa to come and see him about the camping of course. You can't go off with someone he doesn't know. I'm so pleased I met you. I'd better go now. It's nearly lunch-time." They exchanged addresses and telephone numbers and said goodbye. Ravi went home thoughtfully. How lively and interested in things Aman was! Ravi's own life had become such a mess that he was longing for someone who seemed to be happy.

He thought about what Aman had said about being greedy. That applied to everyone. If he hadn't been greedy he wouldn't be in this mess.

Greedy for money. Aman had talked about giving back to Nature. Suppose he gave back the money he had taken from Sumit, Manoj and Madan? Would that make him feel less mean? It would make him look very foolish though. And then there was his father's money. He hadn't in fact spent any of it yet. It was lying in his bed-box just as it was when he took it, but he couldn't replace it because his father kept his wardrobe locked at all times now. Suppose he plucked up courage and gave it back to his father and explained the whole thing, and admit that it was his fault his mother had left? Would his father beat him up?

"Go, on," whispered Merriol, "do it." Normally Merriol let people find their own strength to do what they had to do, but in this case he knew Ravi had become weakened because of poor guidance at home. So he breathed a little of his store of strengthening spirit into the boy's heart. Ravi was amazed! Suddenly he felt he had the heart of a lion!

The evening he went to his father.

"Papa I took that money from your box, not Mummy. Here it is. I haven't used it at all. Please tell me where Mummy is and I'll go and tell her I'm sorry and ask her to come back."

Ravi's father was stunned. That Ravi had taken the money wasn't such a fantastic discovery, though it hadn't occurred to him. But this new Ravi standing straight before him and confessing what he had done was something new! Ravi father felt the stirrings of pride. Of course he had to tell Ravi off a bit because he had certainly been very bad, but that he could behave like a man his Father hadn't suspected. He ended the telling-off with softer words.

"But I'm proud that you have turned out to be such a brave boy. Keep it up son. Now we've got to put all this right haven't we?"

"Yes Papa and I'll give back that money to Sumit and Madan and Manoj, and then I can start afresh."

"Very good. I'll give you the money for that."

"No thank you very much. I'll do that out of my pocket-money."

They talked for some time and Ravi told his Father about Aman. He didn't mention Aman's invitation as he wanted to clean up his life first before he ventured on that. His Father was very pleased about the idea of joining the Sports' Complex though, as he felt healthy exercise would help bring out the best in Ravi. After a while they set off to his in-laws' house. He told Ravi they'd get a big bouquet of flowers on the way, and they'd say they were sorry.

That night Merriol arrived back in Ever-Ever Land tired but happy. The strengthening spirit he had given Ravi would have to be replenished by the Lord of the Universe but it had been well-spent. Ravi shouldn't need any more now that his home was reunited and his parents were helping him in his new life. The Lord of the Universe was satisfied.

"My Ravi should become a useful and happy member of my family now Merriol. Well done."

MERRIOL AND THE LITTLE CAT

There was a storm on Earth. The sky was black except when illuminated from end to end by a bombardment of forked lightening. Rain pelted, window rattled, end hearts trembled. On the veranda of Ben's house there came the forlorn sound of a tiny miaow.

Ben heard it and opened the door. In the corner of the verandah, crouching behind a plant-pot, was a little black and brown cat, not quite a kitten, but less than half-grown. Ben felt very sorry for it all alone in the dark and the storm and it was obviously very frightened. He quickly went to pick up the shivering little animal. Its bones ware prominent after several days' starvation, and it seemed glad to have been found by someone. Ben took it inside and rubbed it fairly dry on an old towel. Then he took it to the kitchen. He broke some pieces of bread into a bowl of milk and set it before the cat. At first the cat seemed as if it could hardly believe its eyes, and approached the bowl cautiously. It investigated the milk and gave it an exploratory lick. "Mmm," it seemed to think, "it's very good." Then it squatted down and proceeded to eat the lot. Ben watched it with satisfaction.

When all the bread and milk were gone Ben brought an old shawl of his Mother's and wrapped the cat up in it, and took it to his bedroom. All this time his parents had been watching T.V. unaware of Ben's rescue act. He sat on his bed with the little cosy bundle on his knee. As the warmth began to penetrate the cat's body it relaxed and in a few minutes Ben heard a low rumbling noise. The cat hai started to purr.

Ben's Mother called out,

"Ben? What are you doing?"

"Come and see Mummy.'" He called. "I've got a kitten."

"You've got a what?" exclaimed his Mother, and she came quickly to investigate.

"What are you doing with my shawl?" She asked. Ben showed her the little cat's face peeping out from amongst the folds. She almost screamed.

"Ben!" she cried, "What have you got there?"

"It's only a little cat Mummy," said Ben. "It had got lost in the storm and it was cold and frightened and hungry. I couldn't leave it outside. I've given it some bread and milk and now I'm warming it up."

"In my shawl! You just put that dirty animal outside immediately. It'll make the house smell!"

"But Mummy it's raining."

"That doesn't matter. Animals are used to rain. I can't have that creature in the house."

Ben tried to argue but it was no good. She wouldn't listen. Weeping in his heart and talking softly to the cat he put it outside on the verandah again. A blast of cold air struck him like a blow. The cat started to miaow again loudly. It had liked the shelter of Ben's house, and after the bread and milk was enjoying settling down to a nice sleep in the warmth of the shawl. It had been as good as being curled up again against the mother's furry tummy.

"There's a cat on the verandah," said Ben's father, coming out of the sitting-room.

"I know," said his Mother. "Ben brought it inside and fed it, and now of course it won't go away again. It'll pester us for days."

"I'll get rid of it," said Ben's Father. He opened the door, letting in another blast of cold air and some spray from the pouring rain. The storm had passed over but the rain would continue for some time. Ben watched in agony as his father picked up some earth from one of the pots on the verandah and thew it at the cat. Immediately the cat disappeared into the darkness.

"I don't know what you were thinking of," complained Ben's Mother, "bringing a dirty thing like that into the house."

"It was cold and wet and lost Mummy," repeated Ben.

"So are all the other cats and dogs out there," said his father. "Are we supposed to take them all in and turn this house into an animal shelter?"

"No but this one was on our verandah like an unexpected guest," and Ben.

"Nonesense," said his Mother. But that night in bed Ben was tormented by the thought of the little cat. It had been so happy and purring in the shawl….. Where was it now? He got out of bed and went to the window. No sign of it. He tiptoed softly to the verandah door and peered through the glass. Yes! There it was huddling into the corner of the verandah again. Softly he unbolted the door and went out. The rain had eased off but there was still a cold wind. The cat gave a little miaow when it saw him. He picked it up, wet again. He couldn't bear it. He took it into the house, bolted the door, and tiptoed back to his bedroom. There was no doubt it was a bit dirty. He closed his bedroom door and rutted it again with the towel. The cat knew it needel a wash and started to lick itself.

Ben sat back with pleasure to watch the small cat lick itself methodically with its rough tongue all over. Ben smiled as it licked its fore-paws and then rubbed them over its face and ears on both sides. The process took some time, and when it stopped Ben whispered.

"Now you're a bit cleaner you can come under my quilt, but only for tonight you know." He sniffed at the cat's fur to see it it smelt very bad, but there didn't seem to be any special small besides damp fur. The cat crapt under the quilt and settled itself, purring, against Ben's back, and in no time both were fast asleep.

In the morning however Ben woke up to the sound of his Mother banging on his bedroom door.

"Ben! Wake up!" she was calling. "What have you locked your door for? Open up!" Ben remembered the cat. He pulled back his quilt and there it was stretching luxuriously and wondering why it had been disturbed. It was as warm as a hot water bottle in its woolly coat. Ben whispered.

"Time to go now puss. The rain's stopped." He opened his window and popped the warm bundle outside. Then he straightened his quilt and hastened to open his door. He hated deceiving his mother but last might his distress for the cat had outweighed other considerations.

"Why did you close your door Ben? Come along now. It's time for your bath." Ben got ready for school.

The next few days however the cat was a constant visitor. Ben put out milk for it whenever he could, but he didn't bring it into the house again. The cat clearly believed it had been adopted and miaowed constantly to be let in. Ben's parents were fed up and said.

"This is what comes of bringing it into the house that night Ben. Now it thinks it belongs here." Ben knew it was useless to ask to be allowed to keep it. His parents didn't like animals. Ben too had grown up in a town but somehow he loved them. He always watched wild life programs on T.V. even it they were about sea creatures he would probably never see in real life.

He hoped though he would one day have the chance to see even them. How thrilling it would be if one day he could do like some of the people on T.V. did and help to save some threatened species! Meanwhile in his own world the little black and brown cat was threatened. Not that his parents would have dreamed of killing it, but they decided it must be moved elsewhere.

Ben's Father put it in his car and said he'ld leave it in another colony of the town to bother someone else.

"It wants to be our cat. Can't we keep it?" asked Ben in a last desperate attempt for the cat.

"Certainly not," said his Mother. "I've heard they bring bad luck apart from anything else."

"They keep away the rats. That's good luck,"protested Ben. "Papa was complaining about the rats eating his books and cats are clean."

"That's enough Ben," said his Mother. Ben's Father drove off with the cat in the back seat and Ben went sadly back into the house. That had been his closest encounter with an animal and he felt he was losing a friend.

Merriol, messenger to Hycarbox, Lord of the Earth, had observed these events. That evening when he returned to Ever-Ever Land after his day's wanderings around the face of the Earth recording events in his heart he opened his tunic for the Lord to see the affair of the little black and white cat. For all the creatures of the Earth came under the authority of Hycarbox, and no creature was so small that he did not acknowledge it as his.

And where is my Nutti now?" asked the Lord, for this was his name for this particular cat.

"He's poking around looking for food about ten kilometers from Ben's house," said Merriol. "But cats are very clever and it will probably find its way back. Ben loves it and animals too like to be loved."

"Yes," said Hycarbox. "I think it will. Nutti's nature has not been hardened yet by the hardness of the world, and he is ready to be adopted by someone who wants him. Now we have another concern here Merriol. Ben is a very special boy. I have had my eye on him since he was a baby and I saw with what concentration he watched the butterflies. I hope to give him very special work when he grows up, and having Nutti would help prepare him. However it isn't good for my children to deceive their parents. And to take a cat straight from outside and put it in bed with him, even after it had washed itself a bit, was not hygienic! An animal which lives mostly in the house in clean enough, but my dear Nutti roves around garbage dumps."

"And what Ben's Father said was right that most animals do live outside," said Merriol.

"Yes Merriol. My animals are mostly children of the elements, and are happier roaming the Earth. But Ben was also right. Because of their well-developed brains human beings have special advantages. They have made thousands of discoveries which they use to make their lives more comfortable and interesting. But they tend to be self-centred. They take what the animals can give, and forgets sometimes to share what they've got with animals. Sometimes animals need food or shelter. Sometimes they need medical care. Ben saw a very young animal separated from its mother and in need of food and shelter and Ben gave them."

"So what should we do Lord?" asked Merriol.

"We have to show Ben's parents that animals too belong to the Earth. They aren't just in the way. His parents are good people. They just haven't stopped to think. That's all."

"What's all that about bad luck?" asked Merriol.

"Ben's Mother didn't study science. All the creatures and plants of the earth share the same molecules and are all related to each other. She thinks animals have nothing to do with her except for their gifts, or as signs. She forgets that a loving heart always brings its owner to a safe harbour in the end. She's afraid, because she doesn't know she's part a of the world and all that lives here. She's afraid of what she sees about her. We have to teach her that animals are her brothers and sisters." Hycarbox smiled.

"But she's an adult. It's going to be hard to teach her to love Nutti!. said Merriol, rather daunted.

"Oh I think we can," said the Lord, "I think we can, and we have to manage it before Nutti returns to them.

"What shall I do Lord"? asked Merriol.

"An old school friend of Ben's Mother lives in a small rural town not too far away from where Ben lives. Ask her to invite Ben's family over this next weekend."

"Yes Lord."

Next morning Merriol went first to Lalkhet to a low rambling old bungalow with a long verandah and a large compound. This was where Breckon, Ben's Mother's friend, lived. Breckon was sitting in a deep wicker arm-chair on the verandah sipping tea and reading the newspaper.

"it's lonely here while your husband is away," whispered Merriol in her ear. "Why not invite Laila this weekend along with Jimmy and Ben?" Breckon could not see Merriol because he was a creature of the air and wind, but she thought to herself,

"It's lonely without Don. It's a long time since I saw Laila. I'ld love a nice gossip with her. I wonder if she could come over this next weekend? They could stay Saturday night."

She went into the house to her telephone and put through a trunk call to Ben's house. It was Ben's Mother who answered the phone.

"Laila?" she heard. "This is Breckon. It's ages since I saw you." They chatted for a minute about their families. Then Breckon issued her invitation for the next weekend. Laila had been wanting a change, and accepted with pleasure, hoping it would be alright with Jimmy, Ben's Father.

When Ben heard about the trip he was thrilled. They had been there before and he knew it meant wanderings through fields, watching the Persian wheel, sailing his boat, and playing with the goats Breckon kept. She also had a beautiful golden Labrador dog called Rex. He gamboled about the farm all day and seemed to understand every word Breckon said.

The next Saturday morning they all set off cheerfully in the car, and arrived a short while before lunch-time. Laila was delighted to see them and showed them to their room. It was very spacious and the three beds were dwarfed in it. Rex galloped towards them to welcome them and put his front paws up on Ben's chest. Ben patted his head and rubbed him behind his ears. When friends came he welcome them, but if anyone came to the gate whose intentions were suspect from his point of view he put his nose to the ground inside the gate and growled a low growl. The visitor had to wait outside till Breckon came. No-one would dare climb over the wall. Thus Breckon felt quite secure even when she was there by herself. When her husband's business took him away Rex was also her companion. Now Rex was very happy because Ben's coming meant fun.

Lunch was served on the verandah and then Ben was free to explore. He wandered along the tracks between the fields with Rex at his heels. When he came to the persian wheel which he had remembered from his last visit he stopped to watch the two bullocks as they circled endlessly round the well. The buckets in the wheel tipped water into a channel which served to irrigate the fields. A farm labourer was squatting on a wall nearby, so Ben asked the man if the bullocks didn't get bored plodding round and round like that all day. The man laughed.

"This is light work," he said, "They might have been pulling carts, and they get their pay in good food. If we go hungry they don't. What about me sitting here? You don't ask if I'm bored!" Ben laughed. He liked the farm laborers with their unhurried ways and their humours, and he stopped to chat with some for a while.

Then he went on to look at the tank where water was stored. It was not deep and the last time he came he had sailed his boat on it. The water was a bit green in places but there seemed to be enough clear water to sail his boat this time too. Some birds were floating lazily on its surface, and Ben thought how nice it must be to be one of those birds. One could float on the water or dive under. And then when one felt like it one could fly off into the sky. He imagined all this so hard that for a moment he felt he almost knew what it was like to be a bird.

Then he noticed the time and realized his Mother would be wondering what had happened to him. He hurried back to Breckon's house, Rex still running around near his feet. Breckon had a large T.V. and in the evening they say watching two or three programmes while Rex snoozed on the carpet beside them. At bed time Rex went out into the compound. Except in very bad weather he always slept outside so that burglars would be afraid to approach. Ben's Mother liked Rex because he was such a beautiful animal and so friendly, but all the same she was afraid to touch him. Ben's Father would pat him and scratch him behind the ear.

The next morning Ben woke early, and when he smelt the cool scented air he remembered he was in Lalkhet and ran to the window. A gardener was already busy among the plant-pots, and a maid-servant was hanging out some clothes. Rex was playing about near the mali, chasing imaginary rats it seemed. Merriol too was about early. He approached Ben unseen.

"It's so lovely outside," he whispered. "You could take Rex for an early morning run and sail your boat before breakfast. Your parents might want to leave early."

"I think I'll go out before breakfast," thought Ben. "I can sail my boat and give Rex a run. We'll be going home in the afternoon and Mummy and Papa might have other plans for this morning." So he slipped into his knicker and T-shirt and got out his blue and white motor-boat, and a red ball he had brought for Rex. It was the right size for him to pick up in his mouth.

"Rex! Rex!" he called as he went down the garden path. Rex bounded towards him and they set off along the lane which led to the fields. Ben tossed the ball ahead as he went, and each time Rex run after it and brought it back and dropped it at his feet. Then Rex would watch expectantly, panting with excitement and tossing his head, eager to run again. Then off he would gallop, ears bouncing as he ran, and his coat golden in the early morning sun. However far Ben threw the ball it was back again in half a minute.

"How lovely if life could always to like this," dreamed Ben. Then he imagined to himself being a dog living here in a rural area with plenty of space, running up and down barking, and then going home to a nice dinner. Soon they came to the tank, and Ben wound up his motor boat and set it on the water. Rex stood at the water's edge panting and wagging his tail. Off zoomed the little boat, its blue and white colours flashing in the sunlight. Ben watched it proudly, and even Rex seemed impressed. He sat down beside Ben. Ben chewed a piece of grass, his eyes on the boat. It came to halt near the opposite corner of the tank and Ben ran round to get it and set it off on its return journey. It was a little too far from the edge to reach so Ben looked round for a stick, but there didn't seem to be a stick handy. So Ben knelt down and stretched out his hand towards the boat. The earth at the edge of the tank was soft and gave way under his knees. The next moment he was in the cold, rather slimy, water. He put his feet down confidently however because this wasn't a deep tank, worried more about his clothes. But to his horror his feet couldn't find the bottom! There was only wet emptiness beneath him. What had happened? He struggled and gasped and tried to reach the bank but he couldn't. His head went under and the horrid dirty water entered his nostrils. He began to thrash out uselessly with his arms, and was on the verge of despair when he felt a solid woolly body immediately beside him. Rex! Dear old Rex. He could swim. He grasped Rex in his arms trying not to struggle or create any more difficulties for the dog, and Rex began to paddle them towards the bank. The big dog had to paddle furiously to keep them both afloat. The bank was only a couple of yards away and in no time Ben was near enough to be able to catch hold of a bit of tree-root sticking out from the earth. He held on to this firmly while Rex scrambled out. The walls of the tank were uneven. It had been lined with bricks which were not in good repair and there were narrow footholds and ledges. So holding tightly to his tree root and searching for footholds Ben too managed to lever himself out of the tank. He collapsed, soaking wet and smelling of pond weed on to the grass.

But oh dear, now there was another problem. The strain of pushing his foot on to one of the narrow ledges in the wall of the tank had caused him to twist his foot and now his right ankle was quite painful. He looked at it anxiously. It seemed to be swelling before his eyes! He tried to get up and put his weight on it but the pain was severe and he flopped down on to the grass again. How was he to get back to Breckon's house. It was already breakfast time and they would all be worried soon if he didn't appear.

Rex however had sized up the situation, and after a pause to watch Ben's efforts to walk he galloped off in the direction of home. Ben sat down. Dogs can show human beings when they are needed and he knew Rex would manage to bring help. Meanwhile he was dreadfuly wet and cold and his boat was still in the tank. The ball was beside him where Rex had left it.

Back at Breckon's house Ben's Mother had been exclaiming about Ben's disappearance so early in the morning without even taking his bath. Breakfast was ready by nine o'clock but there was no sign of Ben. It was such bad manners to be late when he knew Breckon would be serving breakfast! They apologised to Breckon but she said it didn't matter and no doubt Ben had gone further than he intended. Rex was with him and there was no question of Rex getting lost. They sat on the verandah watching the gate, expecting Ben to appear any moment.

They were just beginning to be seriously worried when the golden form of Rex appeared. He scrambled over the top of the gate as was his custom and galloped up the path towards them soaking went. They were horrified to realise that Ben was not with him. They waited for a minute, thinking perhaps that Rex had run ahead and Ben's Mother got up to go and see. Then they realised that Rex was trying to tell them something. He would bound towards them, toss his head, and then run off down the path. Then he would run towards them again, toss his head again and run off again.

"He wants us to go with him," exclaimed Breckon. "I do hope Ben isn't in trouble. Come along." She got up to run after Rex, and Ben's parents in a panic ran too. His Mother was almost in tears.

"Oh what can have happened to him?" she wailed.

"Now don't panic Laila," said her husband but he was running just as hard. They hurried along the lane to the fields after Rex. The big dog ran ahead of them, stopping frequently to check that they were with him.

"He's going to the tank!" cried Breckon.

"But it's not all that deep," reassured Ben's Father. Breckon didn't say anything but she had gone white with fear. The last monsoon had been heavy and since then the tank had been unusually full. She had completely forgotten to warn her friends that been shouldn't go too near. She was aghast at the thought of what might have happened. She began to run as fast as she could towards the tank. When its greenish surface came into view she was even more horrified. Ben was nowhere to be seen! Rex came to a standstill and looked puzzled. He sniffed around and looked up at them, his tail at half-mast.

Ben's parents looked down at the red ball they recognized. Then they saw the blue and white boat bobbing about on the water.

"This is where he was," whispered Breckon. She peered into the water but it was too murky to see much.

"The level of the water is very high this year………." Said Ben's Father slowly.

"Yes……. I forgot to tell you………," said Breckon in a strangled voice,"it's quite deep now."

"Ben!!!" screamed his Mother. His Father put a hand on her arm.

"Wait a minute….see… the earth hare is broken in. There seems to have been some sort of struggle, and the ground here is quite wet." He looked to Rex for answers, but Rex couldn't tell him that Ben had indeed fallen but had managed to climb out again and had lain here on the bank where the wet earth was. Rex's problem was different. Where had Ben gone now? He should have been sitting waiting for them and he had disappeared. There were several interesting scents around the wet patch. He sniffed industriously. He could identify Ben's scent, but there were others, and some earth had been disturbed. He could distinguish the other scents from Ben's and with perseverance he discovered the direction they went from the wet patch. Still snuffling he followed the trail.

"Look at Rex!" said Breakon. "He's not interested in the tank. He's heading that way! If Ben had been in the tank he would have stood looking into the tank or jumped in, but he's showing us Ben isn't in the tank." Ben's Father made to catch Rex up.

"Keep back Jimmy," warned Breckon. "He's following a trail now. We have to keep behind." Laila sobbing quietly hurried along close to Breckon's side. They couldn't go very fast however as Rex kept pausing to make sure of his trail. The three followers kept quiet as if silence might help.

"What on earth made Ben wander this way?" wondered his Father. They had entered the jungle now.

"We can't be many minutes behind him surely," said Breckon. Then they saw a roughly built stone shed amongst the trees. Rex headed straight for it. Then to their utter relief they beared Ben's voice calling.

"Rex! I'm here!" They ran to the shed. It had a tiny barred window and a narrow door with a bar across it. Straining his eyes at the window to see Rex was Ben. Then he saw the others.

"Mummy!" he cried, "Papa! You've found me."

"Ben what on earth are you doing here? What happened?" said his mother. His father had lifted the bolt and opened the door. Ben hobbled out thankful to be out of the dreadful shed.

"Oh papa it was dreadful," he said." I slipped and fall into the tank and it was very deep, not like before. I couldn't reach the bottom and I thought I was going to drown but Rex jumped in and saved me! He really did! I held on to him and he paddled us back to the bank. It was difficult climbing out and that was when I sprained my ankle. Rex saw I couldn't walk very well so he ran off to fetch you. I sat down to wait. I knew he'd manage it. But some men came. Two of them, quite well-dressed. They must have been dacoits Papa! They were quite friendly at first and asked where I was staying, and what my Father did. They must have thought we were wealthy people because they grabbed hold of me and dragged me here. I could hardly walk but they weren't bothered. They were going to claim a ransom! They bolted me in here and left me about ten minutes ago. I thought you'ld never find me here!"

"Rex brought us," said his Mother. "He followed your scent. We'll never forget what Rex has done for us today," she said shedding tears of relief. Breckon too was weeping. How could she have been so thoughtless, she kept thinking to herself. If it hadn't been for Rex the child would have been drowned. She bent down and hugged her dog. Rex just panted and wagged his tail, not understanding what was going on, though he had smelt the trail of the men and had sensed danger.

"Thank you Rex," said Leila, bending down and patting Rex. Rex licked her hand. Encouraged, Ben's Mother too hugged the dog and shed a few tears on his woolly neck.

"Alright, well let's get Ben home as quickly as possible," said his Father. "Climb on my back Ben. You can go piggy-back. Then we'll have to tell the police and you must give them a description of the men Ben."

"We'll go to the doctor first with that ankle," said Breckon."I'll never forgive myself Laila for my negligence. I completely forgot to tell you about the tank."

"You can't think of everything Breakon," said Ben's Mother, " and how were you to know Ben would go off and sail his boat on it"! He's safe now so let's not think any more about that." Ben's Mother did think about the accident of course many times, but there was no point in upsetting Breckon any more than she already was.

They went to the doctor after Ben had changed his clothes and bathed, and then to the police, they finally reached home in time for brunch. Now that his ankle was firmly bound and he had had some medicine for the pain Ben was hungry. After the meal Laila said.

:I wish there was some way we could reward Rex. He has saved our son twice over, and used such intelligence. But what can we do for a dog?" Breckon hesitated, and then said.

"Well, there is one thing. You don't owe anything. The fault was entirely mine. But Rex has a cyst under his back leg which is already starting to irritate him, see?" She lifted the dog/s left back leg and they could see a ball-shaped lump.

"It's getting bigger and needs to be removed. With Don away I'm not able to get him to a vet. It will be a very small operation and a few stitches I suppose. If it would be possible for you to take him back to town and take him to a vet tomorrow that would be a worry off my mind. You could give me a ring as soon as the vet has finished with him and I'll send someone to pick him up. It might mean having to look after him two or three days. Could you bear it?" Ben was thrilled at the very idea, but Laila quaked within. However she felt she couldn't refuse.

"Well.... I'm not used to dogs as you know, and I don't know what sort of a job I'ld make of it... but this is a very special dog and I'ld like to have a go at caring for him." Breckon was delighted. They discussed his diet and Breckon brought his food dishes to take with them. When it was time to go they put Rex in the back of Ben's car and Ben sat with him. Breckon told Laila she had better sit with Rex too to make sure he didn't create any disturbance in the back of the car. Rex, like, most dogs, loved a car ride and tended to get over-excited. Also he had to be prevented from sticking his head out of the window. So Laila got gingerly into the back of the car and grasped Rex's collar as Breckon instructed her, and away they drove. For a while Rex stood watching out of the car window, panting and occasionally barking a little. Then he grew sleepy and lay down with his head on Laila's lap. She stroked his head, admiring the colour of his fur.

"What a beautiful dog he is!" she thought.

The next day Ben's parents took Rex to their local vet. The cyst was removed quite quickly under a local anaesthetic. Leila even held his head while it was done, but he didn't struggle. The vet put in three stitches and placed a wad of cotton wool over them and some tape. They took him home, and then their task was to prevent him pulling off his bandage. Leila found an old knicker of Ben's and made a sheath to tie round Rex's back leg over his bandage. They had to keep Rex a few days till it was time to remove the stitches and the whole family became very attached to him. Ben's Father took him out each night and Ben took him out each morning and his Mother found courage to take him out during the day. He walked so well she enjoyed it and felt proud of the admiring glances at his beautiful coat. When the stitches were removed they rang Breckon to let her know and she promised to send someone to pick him up the next day. When the car came Laila was sorry to see him go and kissed him on the top of his head.

"I thought you said animals were dirty Mummy." was Ben's comment.

"Not Rex," said his Mummy firmly." Breckon keeps him beautifully. Animals aren't dirty in themselves. They only get dirty in dirty surroundings."

"Oh," said Ben, and his Father winked at him.

It was two days later when a miaow was heard outside their front door again. Nutti was back. Ben opened the door to greet him. Nutti miaowed a welcome and rubbed himself against Ben's legs. Ben went to get a saucer of milk for him.

"What are you doing with that milk Ben?" asked his Mother.

"That little cat is back Mummy. I thought I'd just given him some milk at least. He thinks he belongs to us." Laila went to the door to look at Nutti. Now she saw him with completely new eyes. Of course he was quite different from Rex, but now she could see him as a fellow living being, and also beautiful in his own way. Besides it would be very nice for Ben.........

"Hmmmm," she said thoughtfully. "He is rather a nice little cat after all........ bring him through to the kitchen Ben. Let's so if we can find him something more than milk to eat."

"Oh Mummy!" shouted Ben joyfully. He cuddled the cat to his chest and closed the door. "I think you're home now," he whispered in its ear. Ben's Mother started to stroke it cautiously. It began purring and rubbing against her leg.

"It seems to be saying thank you," she said. She gave it a bowl of fish-bits mixed with bread.

"Even if it isn't, I am!" said Ben hugging his Mother. "Will Papa let me keep him?"

"Oh I think so," said his Mother. "Maybe it's time we learnt a bit more about animals, and pussy can teach us."

"Why not call him Nutti?" suggested Merriol close by Ben's ear.

"Let's call him Nutti Mummy,"he said. She smiled.

"Alright. Nutti it is. Welcome home Nutti."

The Lord of the Earth also smiled.

"Poor Ben," he commented. "We made him suffer a lot, but I think if he knew it was all for Nutti's" sake he would be content. As it is he can see the result in his Mother's" change of heart. She had to be brought into a direct encounter with an animal for which she felt an obligation. The rest was the natural impulse of a warm heart. Ben will learn that animals too have individuality, their own idiosyncracies and lovable traits. You have done a good job Merriol."

MERRIOL AND THE OLD LADY

Neena was in class VIII at her school. Her best friends were Lola and Dot. Each week in her school there was a free period when the class teachers discussed with their children some topic of general interest. It might to a national or international issue, or it might be some moral or social question. The teachers told their children what next week's subject would be so that they could be thinking about it in preparation. When the time came the teachers would have some points ready for discussion and the children were invited to say what they thought or knew about the subject. There were a few rules. Each child wishing to speak put up his or her hand. The teacher invited the child to speak and tried to see that each pupil got at least one turn. When invited to speak the pupil stood, and while he or she was speaking there to be no interruptions No-one was allowed to laugh or criticize. The rest of the class must listen quietly and any one who had a comment afterwards raised a hand. In this atmosphere the children enjoyed the class and liked their turn to speak. Even the teacher was not allowed to criticize.

One week the teacher announced that the next topic would be helping other people who were not members of one's own family. The class turned out to be quite lively with the children offering all sorts of suggestions. Then one girl stood up and talked about the Boy Scouts. She said the Boy Scout movement was started by Lord Robert Baden-Powell and they had lots of activities, and sometimes they vowed to do one good deed a day. The girl suggested they could do that. They could decide they would do one act of service every day, such as giving a packet of biscuits to a poor child, or doing the shopping for someone who was sick, or visiting some old person who was lonely.

Neena and Lola and Dot went home that afternoon enthusiastic to start on a programme of one good deed a day. Neena told her Mummy about it, and her Mummy thought it sounded a good idea. So Neena asked,"What shall I do today?"

"You can wash the dishes. The maid-servant didn't came," said her Mother.

"Oh," said Neena disappointed. "Well alright, but actually the idea is to help people other than our own families. But anyway," she added good-naturally, "I'll start my good deeds with the dishes." So she went and boiled some hot water in the kettle and washed the lunch dishes. Then it was time to do her homework. Then she played outside for a while, and after that it was time for dinner and bed. There didn't seem to be much time for one's good deed out side the home when one got down to trying!

The next day at school Lola said she had weeded her neighbour's garden, and Dot said she had taken one of her neighbour's baby out in its pram for a while. These sounded like proper good deeds, thought Neena.

That afternoon she got out her pocket money to see how much there was. Twenty-two rupees. Well she could easily get a packet of biscuits out of that. So she went along the road to the local shop and bought a packet of butter-cream biscuits, her own favorite. Then she went along to some hutments, and seeing a child of about four sitting on the ground near its doorway in a little vest and no knicker, Neena went up to it and said hello. The child started at her, and all the jhuggi-dwellers looked at her wondering what she wanted. So feeling a bit self-conscious she popped the packet of biscuits in the child's hand and went home. It had been an awkward experience, but at least she'll done it and the child would surely like the biscuits (if no one had taken them from him.)

The next day she reported her good deed to Lola and Dot. Lola said she'ld given some toffees to children in their local jhuggies, and Dot said she'll been to visit on old lady in their apartments.

Neena had liked giving the biscuits, but her pocket money wouldn't stretch to many such gifts, so the third day she looked around for something which wouldn't cost money. It should be something for someone outside the family, though, so she walked along the road to the local market hoping for inspiration.

On the way she saw an old woman sitting on the edge of the pavement. She was wearing an old cotton sari and in front of her she had placed a tin for alms. She held out her hand to each passerby. Neena hadn't got any money but she thought perhaps her good deed could be talking to the old woman. So she went up to her and said hello. The old woman peered up at her and asked for money . Neena said she was sorry she hadn't any. She said,

"I haven't seen you before. Where do you live?" The old woman waved her hand dismissively. She didn't want to talk. She just wanted money. How had the old woman got to this state? She must have been a girl too with her parents once. Then she must have been married off. Had she any children? Neena wondered. If so what was she doing in the gutter? Neena tried again.

"Where do you live?" The woman waved her hand again but she said,

"Dillon Bridge."

"Dillon Bridge?" repeated Neena. "You mean underneath it or on top of it?" Dillon Bridge was a bridge over a railway line and a road not far away.

"Near it," said the old woman.

"Who do you live with?" asked Neena. The old woman didn't want to answer that. She didn't want to talk about herself.

"Have you got a room there?" persevered Neena. She knew there were some dark dirty-looking rooms along the road under the bridge. They were rat-infested, and dusty from the traffic and the trains passing regularly.

"No," said woman. "I live with someone there."

"Who?" asked Neena. It was very had work.

"Shanti."

"Is she your sister?" The old woman waved her hand negatively.

"Can I visit you there? Asked Neena. The old woman gazed at her blankly but by now Neena had got into her stride.

"What is your name?"

"Savitri," said the woman.

"I'll come and visit you tomorrow morning by Dillon Bridge, O.K.?" said Neena. The old woman just gazed at her.

It hadn't been much of a conversation but in terms of effort it had been a sizable good deed, and the visit tomorrow, which was Sunday, would be tomorrow's good deed. She had enough money left for another packet of biscuits, so she'd take the old lady some. "Had she any teeth?" wondered Neena. "Yes I think she had."

Dillon Bridge was not far away. The old lady couldn't walk far, so Neena didn't have any difficulty getting there. She took with her the dhobe's nine-year old son, promising him some toffees (out of what was left of her money) on the way back. The road on which she lived led into the main road which passed under Dillon Bridge and it was about fifteen minutes' walk. She set off early so as to be there before the old lady could set off for her begging. When she reached the line of open doorways of the rooms under the bridge she felt very nervous. What sort of people could live in these ghastly places? She was thankful that her papa had a good job and could give them a nice home. She paused by the first doorway, making chhotu, the dhote's son stand with her.

"Is anyone there?" she called. Then she peered in. A woman was cooking something on a kerosene stove. A man was lying on a dari, and a couple of half-clothed children were playing.

"Namasthe-ji," said Neena. "Where does Savitri live?" The woman stared at her, trying to grasp the meaning of a girl like Neena appearing at her doorway before nine in the morning. She knew Savitri however.

"Two doors away," she said. So Neena and Chhotu passed on, mising the next door, and stopping at the second. She peeped inside. Ah yes. There was Savitri squatting on the ground slipping tea out of a tin mug. A younger woman was making rotis. That must be Shanti.

"Namasthe-ji," called Neena again. The two woman looked up. "I've come to visit Sarvitri."

"Savitri?" echoed the younger woman. "Hey! Mata-ji!" she nudged the older woman's knee. "Someone come to see you."

"May I came in?" asked Neena.

"Come in," said Shanti

"Are you her daughter?" asked Neena.

"No, she just stays here," said Shanti,

"How long has she been here?"

"A few weeks," said Shanti.

"Where did she come from?"

"She was staying with some people any they threw her out.

"Doesn't she have any family?" asked Neena.

"Hey! Mata-Ji!" said Shanti . "She's asking if you've got any family".

"There's nobody," said Savitri.

"Who were you living with then?" asked Neena, but Savitri didn't want to talk about it.

"She's very sad, poor thing," said Shanti.

"Why?" asked Neena.

"She has a son but he went away and left her with those people." Neena gazed at Savitri, her eyes beginning to open to the sorrows of the world.

"He was doing well. He didn't want his Mother in the way, I suppose, "said Shanti.

"Where is your son Mata-ji" Neena asked the old lady, crouching in front of her, but Savitri made another negative movement of the hand.

"Is he somewhere near here?"

"Abroad," said Savitri.

"Her son went abroad?" Neena looked to Shanti for confirmation.

"America," clarified Shanti.

"Does he have children?" Neena asked the old lady. She nodded and tears came into her eyes.

"How old are they?" asked Neena, At this Savitri shook her head. She had no idea.

"Do you know how long ago it was that her son went abroad?" She asked Shanti.

"Maybe two years."

She has no idea where he is?" asked Neena. Shanti got up and took down an old cotton bag from a shelf.

"These are her things." Shanti rootled through the contents of the bag and found an old envelope with an address on the back. She showed it to Neena.

"That's where they are." The address on the back of the envelope was in Massachusetts. The local address on the front was c/o a Mr. And Mrs. Kenipat and wasn't far from where Neena lived.

"Hasn't she written to her son?" asked Neena.

"Yes, but he doesn't answer her letters. Now she can't write poor thing. She hasn't got her glasses and she hasn't an aerogramme and she says it's useless writing again anyway.

"I could write to him for you," suggested Neena. "When did your last letter come?"

"About a year ago," said Sarita. "There weren't any more letters after that."

"Where's the letter?" asked Neena. "This is an empty envelope."

"No idea," said Shanti. "That 's all she's got."

Neena studied the envelope trying to memorize the addresses. "Have you got a pencil and paper?" She asked.

"No," said Shanti, but at that moment her husband came in.

"Visitor for Mata-ji," explained Shanti when the man looked at her in surprise. He nodded and Neena greeted him.

"Have you got a pencil please?" she asked. The man had a ball-point pen in his pocket. He lent it to her and Shanti tore a piece of paper off a paper tag. Neena copied down the two addresses and returned the pen. Then she gave Sarita the packet of biscuits and left.

Merriol had been watching these events with keen interest, and reported them back to the Lord Hycarbox.

"So Savitri has found a friend," commented the Lord of the Earth. "I think this needs a little promotion don't you Merriol?"

"Indeed Lord," said Merriol.

"Neena will make her own decisions, but she needs protection. See that she takes someone with her whenever she visits Savitri, and be around to see that she comes to no harm. And her parents must see what she is doing in a benign light, so present to them the good training all this is for Neena."

"Yes Lord."

"Keep an eye on these events for the next few weeks and report back to me."

"Yes Lord."

Neena thought over the problem of Savitri when she got home. The main thing to do seemed to be to contact her son. She thought however that first she would visit the people with whom Savitri had been staying.

"Take Lola and Dot with you," whispered Merriol.

"I'ld better take Lola and Dot with me," thought Neena.

"It's not good to go running round by myself. And then I need an aerogramme to write to her son."

So the next day at school when Lola and Dot reported that they had looked after someone's child while the mother went to the doctor, and done some shopping for an old lady, respectively, Neena told her story about Savitri. Her two friends were amazed that she had gone to the poky quarters under the bridge.

"My Mother would never let me go there," said Lola.

"No. Actually I didn't tell my Mother as a matter of fact, but I took the dhobe's son with me, and after all lots of people live there. How can we say we can't even visit them?"

"Well you can't do much without telling your Mother," objected Dot. "Doing good deeds doesn't mean sneaking off secretly."

"I know," said Neena. "I don't mean to do it again. I wanted to discuss it with you two first and then I'll tell her. What I thought I'ld do is to go to see these people she's been staying with to see what their story is. You never know, she might have just gone off in a huff or something and they're worried to death. And to check up that this is really her son in America or just a story she's told. Then I plan to get an aerogramme and write to him giving news of her. We can all sign so he knows a lot of us know about his Mother what do you think?"

"It sounds a good idea," said Dot cautiously. "I'll go with you if my Mother lets me."

"Alright, well I'll ring you both up this evening to let you know what my Mother says, and if everything's alright we'll go after school tomorrow afternoon."

That evening Neena reminded her Mother about the good deed a day scheme. She told her Mother what she and Dot and Lola had been doing for their deeds, leaving Savitri till the last. She told her Mother how she had met Savitri on the side of the road begging and how she had gone to visit her in the quarter by Dillon Bridge, and the story about her son and about having been thrown out. Her Mother gasped, but Merriol was on hand to whisper.

"See how thoughtful and enterprising Neena has been!"

"She's living with a youngish woman called Shanti and her husband," said Neena. "I didn't like to ask but they seem to have taken her in. She doesn't belong to them. I thought what a very good deed it would be Mummy if I wrote to her son! She says he doesn't answer her letters, but he might if I write. But I thought before writing I should see these people to make sure it's all true. What do you think? I'll go with Lola and Dot, and it's not far away after all. I can just ask if they know an old lady called Savitri and go on from there. I don't think there'ld be any harm would there Mummy?"

Her Mother thought for a few minutes. She had heard what Merriol had said, although she thought it was her own thought. She was proud to think Neena had been able to take all that initiative by herself, and spend her pocket money on someone she didn't even know. However it was risky poking one's nose into other peoples' business. No-one liked it. All the same, this did seem to be a sad case. Neena's Mother herself had a very soft heart and she didn't want to squash Neena's efforts.

"I'll tell you what Neena," she said. "I'll take you in the car. I won't come with you to the house, but I'll wait close by."

"Lola and Dot want to come too Mummy."

"Well they can come here after school tomorrow and I'll take you all. You can handle it in your own way. If when you've talked to these people you still want to write Savitri son we'll get the aerogramme. After the visit the three of you can think what you're going to say."

"Oh thank you Mummy!" cried Neena hugging her Mother.

"But I want you to promise not to do anything without asking me."

"Yes alright Mummy. I promise." Said Neena.

"Next time you want to visit the old lady I'll go too."

Neena rang Lola and Dot to tell them what her Mother had said. Lola and Dot's parents were quite willing to let their daughters join in something Neena was doing if Neena's Mother would be there too, so the visit was fixed for the next day.

As arranged Lola and Dot arrived at Neena's house at four o'clock having had their lunch and changed their clothes. Neena's Mother got out the car and the three girls piled into the back seat. The address on Neena's scrap of paper, now neatly copied into her own address-book, was only five minutes' drive away. The old lady hadn't been strong enough to wander far. The address belonged to a three storied house and the Kenipat family lived on the ground floor. Neena's Mother parked the car opposite the house, and the girls got out and the girls approached the door. They rang the bell and after a few moments a middle-aged lady in a blue sari answered the door.

"Yes?" she said.

"Namasthe Auntie-ji," said Neena. "We wanted to have a word with you."

"Yes?" She obviously wasn't going to invite them in.

"The thing is we've met an old lady called Savitri and she says she used to live here. Do you know her?" The woman paused for a moment. She was thinking quickly and the girls could see she knew Savitri. Otherwise she would have looked amazed. Finally Mrs. Kenipat said.

"Yes she used to stay here but she left." Obviously it was no good saying anything about Savitri being turned out.

"Did you know she has a son in America? She says she has, said Neena. There was another pause.

"Yes she has," said Mrs. Kenipat.

"Well we've been talking to Savitri. She's living in an awful room by Dillon Bridge. She says her son doesn't answer her letters. Do you know if that is so?"

"I don't know anything about that," said Mrs. Kenipat.

"She isn't a relative of yours then?" asked Neena.

"Look – what business is all this of yours? So she's living by Dillon Bridge now. That's her choice. How is it your concern?"

Neena could see that there wasn't any point in pushing the discussion much further.

"Do you know if this is her son's address?" asked Neena. "I wanted to ask that mainly. I thought we might get in touch with him and give him news of his Mother. She needs help. "Neena showed Mrs. Kenipat the slip of paper. She took the paper and looked at it.

"It may be his address," she said. "I'm sure I don't know, and I should keep out of this if I were you. Do you think this man will thank you for poking your nose into his affairs? Wherever Savitri is living she's there by her own choice. I've got my work to do now goodbye." She closed the door. Neena rang the bell again and waited, but Mrs. Kenipat didn't come to the door again.

"Auntie-ji!" she called through the window. "May I have back my piece of paper please?" But there was no response.

"She's kept the piece of paper with the address on it," said Neena.

"I don't suppose she wants you to write to Savitri's son," said Lola. "She'll know you've heard she threw the old lady out!"

"No……," said Neena thoughtfully as they walked back to her Mother's car. "Not that it matters that she's taken the paper because I'ld copied out the addresse." Her Mother was watching for their return and they reported the conversation to her. When they arrived back at Neena's house she drew up by the gate.

"Would you like to come in for a few minutes Lola and Dot?" she asked. "You could draft out your letter. I'll get the aerogramme in the morning and you can copy out your letter neatly after school. Then we'll go and see the old lady shall we? Where does she beg?"

"She was near the market when I saw her, but she's not always there," said Neena.

"I'll get her some more biscuits and some soap," and her Mother.

Merriol reported the day's events to the Lord of the Earth.

"Good," said the Lord. "Now the next thing is to get Savitri to Neena's house. They don't want her where she used to be, and things will be complicated if she disappears from the Dillon Bridge room.

"I'll try Lord," said Merriol.

As promised Neena's Mother got the aerogramme and let the girls write out the letter. They explained that they had met the old lady begging and had gone to visit her in a dirty old room belonging to some people by Dillon Bridge. They said that his Mother said the Kenipats had thrown her out and Mrs. Kenipat said she left of her own accord. They also said Savitri hadn't had any letter from him for over a year, although she herself had written. They sealed their letter and addressed it to Savitri's son and posted it.

When they judged that Savitri would be home after her day's begging Neena's Mother took the girls to Dillon Bridge. They had a plastic bag containing a cotton sari, blouse and petticoat, a few toilet essentials, and some biscuits. They walked as it wasn't far, and Neena's Mother waited at the corner where their road met the main road. The three girls went on to Savitri door. A candle had been lit. The floor was very dusty from the railway grime, and apart from the small area lit by the candle the room was dark. Shanti was busy at her stove as usual, and Savitri was lying on a piece of cloth in the corner. As they went across to her Shanti said.

"She's got fever." Lola put her hand on the old lady's forehead.

"She's burning hot Neena," she said.

"How did she come to live with you?" Dot asked Shanti.

"She sat down to rest under the bridge and I told her to come in. She doesn't eat much and she gets a bit with begging."

"She needs medicine," said Lola.

"Well I haven't got any,"said Shanti.

"You wait here," Neena said to her friends. "I'll go and tell Mummy." Do and Lola crouched down by the old woman who didn't want to talk, while Neena ran back to her Mother.

"Mummy!" she called, Savitri's got very high fever. What shall we do? Come and see." Neena's Mother had wanted the girls to do their own helping as far as possible, but on hearing this she came along herself to see. She entered the small room with a greeting first to Shanti, and a request that she might look at the old lady. Shanti watched events impassively. Neena's" Mother bent down and took hold of the old lady's wrist. It was indeed very hot. She looked round at the grim surroundings and at the old lady on the squalid bit of cloth, and her dirty sari.

"Why not take her home?" suggested Merriol.

"What would her husband think if she took her home?" thought Neena's Mother to herself. Savitri might die here. They could keep her until they got a reply from her son (if they ever did). If nothing happened they could take her to the Missionaries of Charity who had a home in the town for the destitute. The old lady would be clean and well-cared for there. She made her decision.

"Why not take her home?" suggested Merriol.

"Wait here girls," she said." I'll fetch the car and we'll take her home. She might die here and then we'ld feel dreadful. If we don't hear from her son we'll take her to the Missionaries of Charity. I'll be as quick as I can."

""Mummy!" exclaimed Neena. The girls were delighted.

"I'll take her to my place," Neena's Mother said briefly to Shanti. "You've done a lot for her but she needs a doctor."

In a short time she returned and the three girls helped the old lady to the car. Savitri took life as it came and showed no resistance or surprise. When they got home Neena's Mother told the girls to sponge Savitri down in the bathroom with warm water, but to be as quick as possible because of the fever. Then she went and left the girls to cope. She brought a clean nightie and light sweater to dress her in, and then they put her in the spare bed. The girls combed her hair and rubbed oil into her skin. Neena's Mother called the doctor. He checked her over and prescribed medicines which Neena's Mother went to get. By now it was getting late so she drove Lola and Dot home.

When Neena's Father arrived home he was amazed to see their unexpected guest, but Merriol was there to present to him the need for compassion in this case. Savitri stayed in bed several days, but under the doctor's care she was soon well, and Neena's Mother gave her nourishing food. Her husband agreed to help till they heard from the lady's son. Privately he thought they wouldn't hear, but it was clearly their duty to try. The old lady was quiet but they discovered she could read both Hindi and English. Circumstances had reduced her to apathy, but the company of three lively girls soon brought some animation to her face, and she talked a little about her childhood. She was not as old as she had appeared when she was ill-nourished. She had lived in quite a big house in some rural area as a child, but she wouldn't talk about the rest of her life. She felt rejected by her son so she rejected the memories of her married life and her child.

The days passed and the old lady grew stronger. She started to pin up her hair neatly, and in the clean cotton saris Neena's Mother lent her she looked as if she was Neena's Dadi-ji. She started to clean the vegetables and do other light jobs, and to walk in their small garden. She quite liked to watch T.V. She never talked much but she was very neat in her ways. She straightened her own bed and dusted her room, and Neena's Mother rather liked her company. After a fortnight had passed by they started to watch the post every day, but after three weeks had passed they had still had no reply.

Then one evening, just as they were about to start their dinner, the door bell rang. Neena's Father went to open the door, and was amazed to find two policemen standing there.

"We're looking for one Savitri," they said. "Is she here?"

"Why yes!" said Neena's Father, "please come in. Meena!" he called his wife, "the police are here looking for Savitri." The policemen went through to the dinning-room and saw Savitri sitting at the table. At the sight of the policemen she turned pale.

"I must ask you," said one of the policemen, "what Savitri is doing here. We have received a complaint that she was abducted from this address." He showed them a piece of paper on which was written the Kenipats' address. Nenna's Father was outraged.

"Abducted!" he exclaimed. "Quite the contrary. These people threw her out and we rescued her from some hovel under Dillon bridge."

"Well that's the story we have," said the policeman.

"Nonesense!" said Neena's Father. "We've even written to her son in America to tell him she's with us, but we haven't had a reply yet."

"Well your reply is right here," said the policeman. "He's back in India and he's waiting outside in our jeep. He had a call from the Kenipats and came straight away." The policemen went to the door and called out.

"You can come in now Sir! Your Mother is here." Neena's parents rushed to the door followed by Neena herself. They saw a smart young man of about thirty-five getting out of a police jeep at their gate. He came towards them up the path looking angry and aggressive.

"So thanks to the prompt action of my friends we've been able to trace her quickly. Is she alright?" he asked the policemen anxiously.

"You bet she's alright," said Neena's Father, "now. My wife rescued her from a slum under Dillon Bridge filthy and with a raging fever. That was our abduction. See her now." He led them towards the dinning-room.

"Alright, let my Mother speak for herself," said Sarita's son. They all trooped into the dinning-room, and then Neena and her parents stopped in horror. Sarita wasn't there! They rushed through to her bedroom but she wasn't there either!

"She's gone!" said Neena's Father. "She must have taken fright when she saw the police."

"She took her chance to escape you mean," said her son.

"Mybe she did, but it wasn't from the police, it was from you," said Neena's Father. "She'ld just heard you were waiting outside and that you were teamed up with the Kenipats. She won't go back there at any price."

"What you're saying is a rigmarole to me. The Kenipats are close friends and they've been so worried."

"They certainly were," said Neena's Father. Neena and her friends went to see them about your Mother so they panicked."

"Anyway we're wasting time," said one of the policemen.

"Come on. She can't have gone far." Savitri son, and the police, and Neena's Father rushed outside, and chased up and down the road looking for Savitri, but there was no sign of her. Finally they gave up the search, but the police told Neena's parents they must go along to the police-station to give their statement.

Neena was left by herself with the promise that she wouldn't open the door to anyone. Left by herself Neena rang Dot to tell her what had happened, and that Savitri's son had accused her parents of kidnapping Savitri.

"It's a funny story though," said Neena. "Why would my parents want to kidnap an old woman?" But Dot, I wonder if Amma went back to her old quarter. Isn't that where she'ld go? She didn't want to meet her son because she thinks he abandoned her and he'll just take her right back to the Kenipats. I want to go to Dillon Bridge to see but I can't leave the house."

"Neena, wait a few minutes will you?" said Dot."I'll just talk to my parents about it."

After a while the telephone rang and Neena lifted the receiver. It was Dot.

"I've told my parents," she said, " and my Father is going himself to see if she's gone back to that room. He'll just pass by the doorway-I've told him which one- and see if there's an old lady there. He won't say anything.

"Oh fine Dot. Let me know as soon as he gets back. In the meantime I'll ring Lola to tell her what's happened. Dot's Father didn't take long on his errand, and in less than half an hour the bell rang again.

"Neena?" she heard Dot's voice again."Papa says there is an old lady in that room. That must be her."

"Oh thanks Dot. Please tell your Papa thanks from me. I'll wait now for Mummy and Papa to get home and see what has happened at the police-station. I'll ring you first thing tomorrow."

Neena's parents came in very tired. They said they had given their statement to the police but the Kenipats had contradicted it. They said Savitri had been living with them till a fortnight ago when she had disappeared. They had reported her disappearance to the police but had delayed a few days before worrying her son. They said no girls had come to their house saying she had been found by Dillon Bridge and they'ld had no idea where she was. The first clue had come when a neighbour reported having seen her walking in Neena's garden. By then her son was due, so they had waited for his arrival before telling the police and coming to pick her up.

"We need to get hold of Amma to confirm our story," said Neena's Mother.

"Mummy we think she's back in the Dillon Bridge room!" said Neena. "I rang Dot to tell her what had happened and her Father went to see. He says there's an old lady sitting there. It must be Amma!"

"Why yes, of course she'ld go back there,"said Neena's Father. "I'll have to go there right now. We can't risk losing her. Let's all three go and explain things to her and persuade her to go with us to the police-station. She's an adult. She's our guest, and if she wants to stay with us till all this is sorted out the Kenipats can't stop her. If she understands that, I think she will talk to the police. The Kenipats have gone home now and her son's at the Hotel Majestic, so she can see the police privately."

They set off in the car and parked it by the bridge and all three of them approached Shanti's room. Savitri was sitting in the corner again. When she saw them she looked terrified.

"It's alright Amma," said Neena's Mother. "We've come by ourselves. May we come in?" Shanti told them to come in so they went to Savitri and crouched down by her.

"Listen Amma," said Neena's Mother. "The police think we kidnapped you. The Kenipats have told them that, Savitri said.

"Jimmy pays an allowance into my account for my expenses. It's a generous allowance but I didn't get any of it in my hand. Those people took me to the bank to withdraw it each month and were very friendly with all the clerks. But they kept the money themselves. I never got new clothes and I shared the servant's food, and they feed him on cheap rice, dal and roti. Then they started practicing my signature. I just write "Savitri' so it's easy. They tried withdrawing the money on the forged signature with me sitting there in the bank, though they kept me away from the counter. After they had succeeded a few times they threw me out. That was over a year ago. I don't know what happened after that. I didn't want to go back. They ill-treated me a lot. Shanti treated me well, and the food she gave me was quite as good the food the Kenipats gave me. It was a shocking thing to beg, but it was my only way of contributing to Shanti's expenses. I'll go with you to the police to tell them. You've been so kind. I can't let you suffer for it." She got to her feet and told Shanti she was going with her friends.

"You must stay with us Amma till everything is sorted out," said Neena's Father. "No-one can force you to stay with the Kenipats you know, and when your son realizes how they've treated you he won't let you. He came immediately he heard you were lost. He says he got no letter from Neena but he changed to a new flat recently."

They drove straight to be police-station and Savitri told her story. The police summoned her son from his hotel. When he arrived he hugged his Mother and asked her what all this was about. She told him about her miserable time with the Kenipats. He was so shocked he could hardly believe his ears.

"And you say they forged your signature Mother?"

"Yes son,"

"We must go to the bank first thing tomorrow Inspector." He said, "I've had several calls from the Kenipats over recent months saying Mother was having treatment for arthritis. The said she couldn't come to the phone. They wanted extra money to cover her costs. I pay the money through the bank. I thought the expenses were a bit steep, but I trusted them implicitly, and I had told them she must have the best medical treatment whenever it was necessary. They're distant relatives of ours. My father educated Mr. Kenipat. I've known him all my life. Even if they took the money how could they be cruel to my Mother! That's what stuns me. The whole story is incredible. And you even had to beg in the gutter Mother?" He shook his head trying to assimilate all the dreadful facts. Finally he turned to Neena and her parents.

"Well I owe you a big apology, and the biggest possible thank you. And it was you Neena who found my Mother, and went to the trouble of visiting her? And then you all took her in like your own Mother and cared for her?"

"We enjoyed it,"said Neena's Mother.

"I'm very sorry I didn't get your letter. It will have been forwarded to my new address by now. I took a new apartment recently."

Savitri had tears in her eyes.

"Anyway don't cry mama. I've been promoted, and this new flat is more spacious. I'll take you back with me. The children will be thrilled to have their Dadi-ji with them, and Bulbul (that's my wife" he told the others)" was very upset when she heard you'ld disappeared. She told me to be sure to find you and bring you back with me. So they're all waiting for you."

Savitri started to weep with joy, and even Neena had tears in her eyes.

"Well all that's very satisfactory Sir," said the Inspector, "but we'll have to go into this forgery business."

"Yes I suppose you will, but I won't make any charges. It'll be better for us just to forget all this and let Mother start her new life as soon as possible."

"And beta, we mustn't forget Shanti," said Savitri. "She also took me in and saved my life, and the food she gave me was the same as all the family was having, and she gave me milk sometimes.

"What would you like me to do for Shanti?"

"Her husband doesn't have a proper job. Can you get him one?"

"Yes….. I can surely do that. I've got a lot of friends round here. I'll be able to get him fixed up somewhere when they hear what he's done for you."

Merriol waited till they had all left the police-station before returning to the Lord Hycarbox. When he reported the successful outcome of the mission the Lord was very happy.

"See what good can come from a simple wish to do good in a human heart? It finds its response in my heart and summons my help. I'm very pleased with all this Merriol. See that Shanti's husband does get that job, and I think a letter to the principal of Neena's school relating the story and praising Neena, Lola and Dot for their initiative and there compassion would be reward enough for these girls don't you think. And it will inspire others to be alert to the needs of those around them. Now go and rest my Merriol."

MERRIOL AND THE BIKNOR DEMONSTRATION

One evening when Merriol, messenger to Hycarbox, Lord of the Earth, returned to Ever-Ever-Land to report on his day's adventures, the Lord seemed to be preoccupied. He saw what Merriol had to show and listened to his observations and his report, and then he said,

"Merriol a new danger is developing at a fast rate for my children. In the cities, as you know, the fumes from the motor vehicles and industry have made the air most unhealthy for human beings and plants and animals. Human beings know this but they aren't prepared to do very much about it. Having a car seems more important than breathing clean air. And they are so beguiled by the new luxury goods produced by their industries that these mean more to them than their health and he future of their planet!"

"Can we not do anything about this Lord?" asked Merriol.

"I don't think so. Their choices are not within my jurisdiction. I can only engineer crisis situations in which the need to make some positive choice is unavoidable. I present certain people with the truth, but the choice they make in the situation is their own. Of course I do evolve situations in which the choice for health and healing is attractive for people who already have some inclination towards me. Where the will is weak we put a little of my strengthening spirit sometimes, but usually I build on firm foundations. Then such people have a positive influence in their society."

"But we do so little Lord."

"Apparently it isn't much, but what I bear in mind is that one strong and generous heart can achieve miracles. The history of the world had many such instances. Florence Nightingale was one. Vivekananda was another. But the numbers are countless. With the weak and the self-centered I can do very little and they form the majority. So we have to select our individuals very carefully Merriol. They are our heroes and heroines who will inspire the many, I can't save the Earth, but I am Lord of its molecules and have power from within."

"But what if they destroy the Earth Lord?" Hycarbox sighed. "You and I will go on Merriol and try again. A new formation of molecules and atoms will evolve... but let's not think of that. Let us hope for the victory of this present Earth. Let us hope for the development of a harmonious interaction of the molecules of the Earth and the Love which over-rules us all."

"You spoke of a special concern Lord?" said Merriol.

"Yes Merriol. These fumes our people would rather inhale than make the smallest sacrifice… the little ones are developing asthma at an alarming rate. The first action of a human being is to draw a breath, and the last action is to draw his last breath. Breathing is the action they take for granted all their lives. One of the most terrible calamities is to have this function disturbed. Now thousands of children are developing asthma Tears came to Merriol's eyes as he thought of these children.

"They are helpless victims Merriol," said Hycarbox,"and we must do something."

"What can we do Lord?" asked Merriol.

"Go to my child Danny. He has a small sister Teena who has got asthma. She is only four years old. Danny is twelve. He watches her anxiously every time she has an attack. Near where Danny lives in Biknor there is a factory. It pours out black smoke into the air, and poisonous waste materials into the river. The owner has received notice to get rid of his obsolete machinery and install modern equipment but he is ignoring the notice. Danny has learnt at school about the harmful effect of fumes and he is angry on account of his sister. We will help Danny to direct his anger usefully. It will be a small achievement, but large achievements grow out of small ones."

Danny was playing cricket in his garden with two of his friends. He lived in a small bungalow on the road connecting the small town of Biknor with the nearest big city. A lot of heavy traffic passed along the road and all the housewives complained about the dust and smoke. The main object of the peoples' resentment however was the chemicals factory down by the river not far from Danny's house. Danny was a fit and healthy boy and had grown up ignoring these problems. If the furniture and curtains were perpetually dirty he was not one to worry about such things. It wasn't until his sister Teena was born that he ever gave the dust and smoke from the nearly factory a serious thought. She was a fragile child from birth, dainty and pretty, but by the time she was two years old she had developed a serious chest complaint. She would wheeze and struggle for breath and sometimes she had to be rushed to the hospital for oxygen. The doctors gave her all the medicines available, but they warned Teena's parents that they should move away from that area. However Danny's father was manager of a local garage and he was afraid to leave his job. His mother taught in a local private nursery school, but they couldn't afford to take Teena away on holiday even. As it was her medicines were very expensive.

Danny heard all the talk about these problems between his parents and their neighbours and friends. They all agreed that Biknor was a very dirty town and those who weren't already suffering from chest or skin problems could expected to do so at any time. They were all annoyed with Mr. Goldbag, the owner of the factory, for not complying with the regulations, but no-one actually did anything. Danny suggested to his father that they make a complaint to Mr. Goldbag about his factory. His father just said Mr. Goldbag was very wealthy and powerful and no-one wanted to antagonize him. Danny thought this was a feeble approach to a public nuisance. As he knelt at his window watching the black smoke rising into the sky Merriol came to him and whispered,

"Discuss this with your friends."

"I think I'll talk to Larry and Neeta about it," thought Danny. " If the grown-ups are afraid to complaint I'm sure we children aren't."

So that evening when the three of them set off down to the river as they often did, Danny launched into the subject.

"Let's go and look at the back of Mr. Goldbag's factory where he throws out his wastes into the river. The smell is so bad there and blows into the town when the wind is in the right direction, or I should say the wrong direction."

"There aren't any fish in the river now," said Neeta. "My Papa says there used to be a lot."

"And ducks and other birds used to float on the river too and I've heard people went boating. Now who wants to go near all this muck?" said Larry.

"Well I've been thinking about it," said Danny. "Teena's got asthma and the doctors say she should get away from all these fumes, but Papa can't give up his job. Every time Teena has a bad attack it makes me furious to think of Mr. Goldbag. What does he care? And I've read in the paper that asthma is becoming much more common. I'm determined to do something about Mr. Goldbag!". This was fighting talk and his friends were impressed. They went along the bank of the river and sat down to talk. The water shone with all the colours of the rainbow because of its oily surface. They watched the black smoke which even now was billowing into the sky.

"Mr. Goldbag may have a lot of money," said Danny, "but he is also a human being. Suppose it were his child who had asthma?"

"He could afford to send him or her away to the hills or somewhere," said Neeta.

"Why not try publicity?" whispered Merriol who was close by.

"We need publicity," said Danny.

"What sort of publicity?" asked Larry.

"I don't know yet," said Danny," but we see all the time how people get themselves into the newspapers when they want something done."

"How?" asked Neeta.

"Well by a demonstration or procession or a stunt," said Danny.

"What could we do that people would be the least bit interested in?" said Dave. "We've only children and our parents would stop us even before we'ld started."

"Well we won't be doing anything wrong,"said Danny. "We would only be exercising our democratic right. And I've got an idea. We'll get as many children to join us as we can and swear them to secrecy. We'll do a demonstration in front of the factory in gas-masks!"

"Gas-masks!" exclaimed Larry.

"Where are we going to get gas-masks from?" said Neeta.

"Oh they won't be real ones of course. We'll make them ourselves. We'll need black cloth and tins. Each child would need to contribute a tin about three inches deep and about four inches across. We'll each pool some of our pocket money to get the cloth and we'll need a girl who's been taught to sew to help us to cut out the hoods and stitch them up. We'll paint the tins black and put little holes in the bottom to form the nose and mouth pieces like there are in gas-masks. Then we'll cut eye-holes in the hoods and attach the tins to cover the nose and mouth. We'll sit in front of the factory wearing our masks pretending we need oxygen because of the fumes. And we'll paint large placards with our slogans."

Larry's eyes sparkled but Neeta looked dubious.

"But who will be impressed?" she asked, "just a few passers-by who will laugh at our children's games."

"No. Everyone knows this is a real issue," said Danny. "I don't think they'll laugh. But in any case we have to tell the newspapers beforehand. That's what people do, so that the papers send their press-photographers. The whole point is to get our picture in the papers with our placards."

"I think it's great idea," said Larry, "and my cousin works for the 'Daily Reporter'. We'll get him to use his influence, and then we can tell other papers that the 'Daily Reporter' man has promised to be there. That'll make them keen not to miss anything. And there isn't much to report on round here. We'll be giving them some excitement."

"Good," said Danny. "Alright then. It's your job to contact your cousin and ask his advice on getting in touch with other papers."

"First we need to fix the date," said Neeta.

"Let's make it a week next Saturday," said Danny .'We'll be on holiday so that will give us ten days for our preparations. I'll round up some children including someone who can sew. I'll tell them to bring a tin each. And we need a small contribution from their pocket money. I'll get a tin of black paint. We'll do the work together somewhere here by the river. It's pretty quiet. Now not a word to anyone except the children who join us. I'll call a meeting in the park next Saturday evening."

Merriol reported these events to the Lord of the Earth.

"Now," said the Lord, "this has to be carefully planned. They need children who will take the job seriously. I suggested the following." The Lord gave Merriol a list of twelve children, including Danny's own.

"Suggest these names to Danny, and be present when he gives the invitations to help persuade them. Keep an eye on things generally so they don't have too much outside interference, and see they don't do anything really foolish. We don't want casualties. You will be kept very busy over the next week Merriol. This sort of thing attracts trouble-makers, and frauds with other motives, and all such people must be kept out of Danny's plans. Keep your eyes and ears open all round. You need not report back here if your presence is needed there, but return as soon as you can."

Merriol was indeed very busy for the next two days. By the time Danny's and Neeta's and Larry's discussion was over it was nearly dark so they had to go home. Merriol visited Danny in his bedroom as he was making out his list of helpers and dictated Hycarbox's list to him. Such was Danny's inner communication with the world of Nature that he responded easily to what Merriol had to say. He placidly wrote down all the names Merriol gave him and stopped when Merriol said,

"That will be enough."

The next day when Danny set off on his bicycle to visit the people on his list Merriol was at his side. A key member of the group was Sindy. She was a sensible girl of thirteen who would be able to calculate how much cloth they would need and how to cut out the hoods. She said she would certainly come to the meeting on Saturday and she would buy the cloth and cut out the hoods. She told Danny how much the cloth would cost and promised to bring her sewing-box on Saturday. She also suggested cutting out skulls and crossbones to stick on the backs of the hoods.

Danny was delighted with all this positive help. He managed to contact all his invitees in two hours, and with the help of Merriol persuade them to be at the meeting in the park, if possible with a tin.

He went home elated. As he entered the door he heard Teena wheezing again. His eyes hardened. The resolve was born in him to make the world a cleaner place to live in. He'ld heard there were courses in environmental studies and his private resolve was do one of these.

However for the present he had plenty on his hands. He had collected fifty-six rupees so far, and the rest was promised. He hunted round the house and discovered at the back of a cupboard an old empty tin.

The next Saturday evening all twelve children gathered excitedly under a tree in the local park. Passers-by saw them and wondered vaguely what they were up to, but Merriol was there to cloud their attention. Merriol had to concentrate his own attention also on keeping the children serious so that the meeting didn't become a party. Danny's sense of purpose was firm and the others soon caught his mood. He spoke first about the purpose of the demonstration and his own personal motivation in Teena's asthma. Teena was not the only sufferer he pointed out. They all knew of people with skin allergies or respiratory infections caused by pollutants in the air, and they had read about them in the newspapers. He outlined his plan for the demonstration.

"Our plan should be simple," he said. "We will meet by the Plaza cinema and march in twos to the factory. The leading pair and last pair will carry the placards. We will walk quietly because it will be our gas-masks and the placards which will make the impression. We are a silent warning. To get people to take us seriously we must behave seriously and sit quietly when we get there. No giggling please."

"How long are we going to sit there?" asked one girl.

"All day," said Danny."I suggested we get there by nine o'clock and stay till six in the evening."

"Suppose the police tell us to go?" asked another.

"Then we'll walk along around carrying our placard. They can't stop us doing that. They can't really stop the demonstration after all. And we're going to have the press there. Larry would you tell us please about your progress?"

"Yes, well I went to see my cousin on the 'Daily Reporter'. I made him promise to see that one of their photographers comes. He knows lots of reporters of course and he said he would get representatives from five or six papers there. I'll see him again later in the week and if there's any doubt about it stand with him while he rings them up, but I think he means to do it."

"Fine," said Danny. "Now we've got here a dozen tins and the black cloth. What do you suggest we do Sindy?"

"I've brought scissors and measuring tape, and I've planned out how to cut the cloth, so I'll do shall I do it?"

"Yes please do," said Danny. They all watched as she folded the cloth and cut it into twelve pieces.

If you like Nan and I will stitch them. We're used to this sort of thing, and if anyone made a bosh of it we'ld only waste the cloth," said Sindy. "We'll draw skulls and crossbones on paper to stick on the backs of the hoods."

"O.K. thanks," said Danny," and the rest of us will paint the tins, and make tiny holes in the bottoms. I'll bring the tins round to your houses by Monday evening. Then please deliver the tins to Sindy by Thursday, for them to be fixed into the hoods. And you'll also stick on the skulls and crossbones won't you Sindy?"

They all agreed to their tasks.

"And we'll meet outside the Plaza cinema at quarter to nine next Sunday morning. O.K.? Any other points?"

"Yes- what about our lunch?" asked someone.

"Oh yes," said Danny. "That's a bit of problem. We'ld look jolly funny in our sinister black hoods stuffing bits of food underneath."

"We can go away one at a time to a quiet corner," suggested another.

"Alright. We'll see what we can do when we get there. Each bring something small for lunch in your pockets. We'll have to bring water-bottles. There's no other way out. I'll bring some drinking straws so we can drink without lifting the hoods."

Merriol returned to the Lord Hycarbox to discuss the developments. The Lord smiled.

"See what splendid training we are giving these young people in co-operative action for a public purpose! This is only the beginning for some of them. But there's still plenty of work for you Merriol. The children must be watched over the whole of next Saturday. On Friday make sure Danny tells the local police about his demonstration. They need a couple of men on duty outside the factory. Be there when he goes to the police and see that the police take a tolerant view of the plan. On Saturday you will be very busy. First you have to see that all the parents' attention is slightly dulled so that there isn't a hue and cry! Then be on duty at the factory. You know the strategy. The planning of the actual demonstration we can leave safety to Danny and Sindy and all the others. Let them work it out for themselves as far as possible. Our guidance is only general. Oh, and see that the press fulfill their promises. That's crucial of course. And they should be there early."

"Yes Lord."

The children were very busy during the next week. Denny and Larry and Dave painted the tins. On Tuesday they delivered them to the others for the making of the holes. The tins were delivered to Sindy on Thursday. She and her friends had been busy with the sewing and on Friday they fitted the black tins in the spaces left for the nose and the mouth. The white skulls and crossbones had been glued to the backs of the hoods. The overall effect was very good they felt.

On Saturday morning as planned they all met outside the Plaza cinema a little surprised at how smoothly their departures from home had gone. The major risk had been a parental intervention at the last moment, but all the parents had been agreeable, if a little absent-minded, about their off-springs' demonstration. Each child had a water-bottle and Danny had the drinking-straws. And each of them had a small lunch-pack tucked away in a pocket.

Danny and Rita and Larry had prepared two large placards covered with white paper. On them they had printed in large black letters "LET THE CHILDREN BREATHE CLEAN AIR", and "WE DON'T WANT CANCER: WE DON'T WANT ASTHMA". They had also painted drops of blood round the words. Danny and Sindy led the procession carrying the first placard, and Larry and Neeta brought up the rear carrying the second placard. They walked silently in twos, letting their appearance carry their message. They certainly drew attention. Passers-by stopped and gazed at the silent procession. A number of other children tagged on behind to join the fun and Larry said sternly through his hood, "If you want to come with us come quietly." Merriol was also around disciplining their followers who contributed to the impact of the procession. By the time they reached Mr. Goldbag's factory they had a strength of two dozen children. They placed the placards against the factory wall and sat down in front of them. The other children sat too, at least for some time. The policemen ambled up and made a few jokes. The children answered politely, but showed they weren't in a mood for foolery.

It wasn't long before Mr. Goldbag got news of the demonstration. He was still at home but set off to the factory at once when the message came. By the time he arrived at half-past nine there were twenty-eight children with the twelve in black gas-masks. When Mr. Goldbag saw the placards he was furious.

"What do you mean by this!" he shouted. "What do you know about running a factory? The country wants chemicals and then complains about the inconvenience of making them!

He was nicely into his stride when the first members of the press arrived. They were quick to appreciate the scene and had taken photographs before Mr. Goldbag was able to take his attention from the children. Several of Mr. Goldbag's men were around watching and Mr. Goldbag was about to order an assault on the pressmen to get hold of their films when the two policemen stepped forward. Mr. Goldbag stormed off into the factory and the children sat silently on. The policemen could make no objection about such a disciplined protest. Few adult demonstrations were organized so well. The extra children identified with aims of the demonstration and took it seriously. The large placards coloured in white and black and red were impressive and the gas-masks looked well. There were small slits for the eyes and the black tins had been fixed in neatly. Eight members of the press arrived. They photographed the group and the placards and asked the children questions. Danny was the spokesman and he explained about the nuisance caused by the factory. He referred to the health hazards it caused in the neighbourhood by its black smoke and the poisonous effluents in the river. He made his points briefly. Merriol whispered to him that the newsmen would unearth all the background themselves. Thus their protest, though modest in scope, got across its main message. The visual impression was good and the fact that the children had organized their protest on their own and done everything themselves made good copy for the reporters. They returned to their offices later in the morning well-satisfied. The police stayed on.

Danny planned to lead his procession back promptly at six so they would all be home before dark. Merriol stayed with the children all day and escorted them back to the Plaza cinema in the evening. Merriol stayed with the children all day and escorted them back to the cinema in the evening. The police too followed behind. At the cinema the children took off their gas-masks and gave them to Sindy to look after in case they were needed again. Merriol flew this way and that seeing them all home. All, that was, except Danny, Neeta and Larry.

They stayed behind to discuss the success of the day. The police-men had a few jokes with them and departed. Then two factory men drew up in a car in front of the cinema and called to the boys.

"Hey!" they said. "Mr. Goldbag would like to discuss things with you. Come with us in the car."

Flushed with the success of their day, as the children were, they were off their guard, though it had not occurred to them that Mr Goldbag might harm then. That wouldn't be democratic after all. Danny even, for a fleeting moment till common sense rebuked him, visualized himself discussing the future of the factory with its owner, man to man! The three children got into the car and were driven back to the factory. They were met at the door by some more men who grabbed hold of them and hustled them along a corridor. Then they were taken down some steps into the basement. In the basement there several rooms were used for storage. There was a big service lift to transport materials to other floors of the factory when they were required. Another room was smaller and contained a desk and a chair. It was into this room that the children were pushed. Nothing was said, the men closed the door and the children could hear them bolting it   and placing a padlock on it. They were prisoners!

The children were dumfounded but Mr. Goldbag's plan was simple. He wanted to punish the children.

For a few minutes they sat on the floor looking at each other trying to make some sense of what had happened to them.   Maybe the men would come and release them when Mr. Goldbag felt he had made his point? It was all very frightening. Whatever the plan was there didn't seem to be anything they could do about it. They looked around the room hopelessly for a while. Then Danny's eyes alighted on the electric mains switches…..

"The switches!" He almost shouted. "They've put us in with the electric meters! Come on. Bolt the door on the inside. Both bolts." Quickly they pushed up and pressed down the two inside bolts.

"Now…" said Danny. They examined the various levers and decided which was the master lever which would switch off the current to the whole factory. By now it was dark outside and the factory worked through the night. It was ablaze with light. The next moment it was eclipsed in darkness. Danny had pushed up the master lever. For a moment everyone thought it was a normal breakdown but the next moment the lights went on again. Everyone sighed with relief, only to find themselves plunged in darkness again. Danny pulled down the lever and the lights went on again. Then he pushed it up and the lights went off. Then he pulled it down…… and so on and so on. Everyone ran to the windows to see if the same things were happening outside, but the street lights were burning steadily, and the lights in the nearby houses were also on. The problem seemed to be limited the factory. Of course only Mr. Goldbag and his helpers knew what was going on down in the basement and he started to curse. He called the men to come with him to the basement and they'ld deal with the nuisance children!

The nuisance children however had had another brainwave. Like most children they knew about the morse code and the famous SOS or 'Help' signal. Three long flashes, three short flashes, three long flashes. It was Neeta who thought of this and immediately Danny changed the length of his times on and off to the Morse SOS signal. People out in the streets by now were very interested and had stopped to watch the show. Even in the houses opposite people were watching from their windows. What next? The factory had certainly had a lively day!

"We can keep this up indefinitely," said Danny happily. "Would you like a turn now Neeta?" Neeta very much would and she took over. By now Mr. Goldbag and three other men had arrived. They unlocked the padlock and drew back the bolt, only to discover that the door was locked from inside! They banged on the door.

"Open the door!" they bellowed. "Stop that at once! Open the door!" But Danny and his friends meant to stay there until help came from outside.

By now the whole neighbourhood was agog! Someone had called the police and someone had rung up the electricity department and someone had rung the local newspaper. The editor, when he heard about this new development, rang his colleagues on the other papers which had been involved in the day's events. This was not an occasion for exclusive scoops! Representatives from the various papers rushed back to the scene. In the meantime a jeep arrived full of uniformed policemen.

Mr. Goldbag was nearly tearing his hair out! He had sent for the electrician to find a way to cut off the current but the man had gone home long ago and had to be fetched. His arrival coincided with that of the police, so he hung about on the outskirts of the crowd to watch developments. The lights were still flashing ON ON ON off off off ON ON ON. He scratched his head in bewilderment. In twenty-two years of service he had never encountered a defect like that before! He didn't know the Morse code but the policemen did and demanded an entry into the factory. The pressmen, who were beginning to arrive, crowded in behind and they all trooped into the factory. The officer in charge asked to be taken down to the meter switches room. There was nothing else for it. The policemen had to be take down to the basement.

The press were very excited to realize just how big a story they had been granted that day. There was Mr. Goldbag himself banging frantically with both hands at the door of the meters room, beside himself with rage! In the flashing of the lights he did not notice the extra flashes caused by press cameras when the factory lights went on! Nor did he or the other men see immediately that some men in uniforms were on the scene. That is until a large hand descended on his shoulder.

"What's all this Mr. Goldbag?" enquired an official voice. He looked round in horror to find himself surrounded by policemen, and, of all things, men with cameras!

"Who is in there Mr. Goldbag?" enquired the officer pleasantly. "Have you got a prisoner or is someone playing tricks?

"Oh it's just some children having a lark," he said angrily. "No need for all this fuss. Just wait till I get my hands on those kids. Open the door!" he bellowed.

"What children?" asked the police officer.

"Danny something and two of his friends," said Mr. Coldbag.

"You mean the demonstraters!" exclaimed one of the policemen who had been on duty earlier.

"Yes that's right," admitted Mr. Goldbag.

"What are they doing down here?" asked the police officer.

"Oh… well… I wanted to talk to them," mumbled Mr. Goldbag.

"Down here in the basement? Anyway they'ld better come out.

Danny!" he called through the door. "We're the police. Open the door."

Inside the three children paused from switching the lights on and off.

"It might be a trick," said Dave.

"How do we know you're the Police?" called Danny.

"May I speak to them Sir?" said one of the policemen, I was with them during the demonstration."

"Please do."

"Hey Danny!" he called. You remember me. I was on duty during your demonstration and went with you back to the Plaza.

Inside the room the children looked at each other.

"That's right," said Larry. "Better open the door." The children were met by a battery of flashlights like film-stars stepping out of their limousines at film festivals.

"Mr. Goldbag and his men locked us in here Sir," said Danny," so we thought of this way of getting help."

"The Morse code," said the police-officer. "Well done all of you. But why did you lock them up in here Mr. Goldbag?" Mr. Goldbag did not want to answer this question. He had been thinking about a good punishment.

"Well in any case I will arrest you for abduction," said the police-officer. "Come along all of you. We'll need statements from you children and then someone can take you home."

Merriol returned some hours later to the Lord of the Earth. The Lord Hycarbox was delighted. He rubbed his hands.

"So the story in tomorrow's papers will be much better than the children ever dreamed! It's worth a front page spread and I'm sure it will get it, along with photographs of the demonstration, and Mr. Goldbag in a rage. Then there will be the photographs taken down in the basement of the factory with Mr. Goldbag hammering at the door of the electric meters room, and then the children emerging! All first-class stuff. Mr. Goldbag will be in police custody for some time, so his son will be able to take over the running of the factory. I think we can look forward to some changes in that neighbourhood. He won't want to hang on to all that obsolete machinery. He's a young man with a bit of vision, just waiting for his chance to make improvements in the running of the factory. Now's his chance to do the stream-lining and landscaping he had been dreaming of."

"And the children didn't suffer too much," commented Merriol.

"Not they. If you were to ask them now they would say they enjoyed it!" smiled the Lord Hycarbox. "I have noted at least five of the twelve in the demonstration who I think will be determined enough to work towards the harmony which is our goal. Go and take some rest now Merriol, and well done."

OTHER BOOKS BY THE SAME AUTHOR:

"SONNY GOGO TOBO

AND

THEIR ADVENTURES"

Lightning Source UK Ltd.
Milton Keynes UK
UKOW07f1203040117

291345UK00010B/34/P

9 781491 889923